A Measure of Happiness

Anne Mason

A family of Millwrights:

Disinherited
A Measure of Happiness

1

Two men stood in the doorway of a cottage in the confines of a millwrights' yard. Around them men were working with wood and at the far end of the yard a furnace glowed red where the ironworks took place. It was noisy.

'I'm telling you, it's not good enough!' James Spandler pointed to the bench next to the door. His brother, Robert, looked exasperated.

'It's got to be,' he threw his hands up into the air, 'because it's his third attempt and he says he's not doing it again.' James moved his face closer to Robert's, stared into his eyes and spoke very quietly.

'You would not pass any other apprentice with work like that. And besides, he's not hung it yet?' Robert lowered his gaze. 'Ah, I see,' James drew a deep breath, 'you are not going to make him hang it. Perhaps you don't want him to because you know it is not fit for purpose?' Robert shrugged. On the bench was a cog wheel which was designed to be mounted on an axle and would mesh with another cog wheel; they were often of different sizes or operating at different angles and needed to be very accurate for a mill to run smoothly. Robert and James owned the millwrights' yard and Robert was the master-in-charge. Their nephew, Henry, watched from the other side of the yard.

'Edmund has been an apprentice for many years. My Mary says he's too old and it humiliates him.'

'Mary is not the master-in-charge. You are. It's your decision. You can call him a millwright if you want but don't expect me to agree with you.' Abruptly James turned away; as he did he caught Henry's eye and there was a tiny shake of his head which Henry saw but Robert didn't. Henry knew; he turned, picked up his axe and removed branches from the tree-trunk by his feet with a ferocity that caused others in the yard to look at him. He did not notice their stares.

Later, as the men were packing up, Robert came over to Henry.

'Come to the King's Arms with me. There's something James and I want to talk to you about.' Henry nodded. He had no doubt as to what it was about.

Later, as he left the King's Arms, he found that the ale had fuelled his anger.

Edmund! Can Robert not see that he shouldn't make him a millwright until he has proved himself, just like everyone else? He has enough of a sense of his own importance and now Robert is going to make it clear to him – and everyone else – that Edmund is privileged. That would be bad enough if he was a talented millwright who worked hard but he is neither of those things – he is fat, lazy and just can't do the job – but he will inherit the position of master-in-charge. That position should have been mine. Damn my father. If he hadn't sold his share Edmund would just be a nuisance and it would not matter that he was incapable. Grandfather was so proud of the yard he had set up – and in the future it will be in Edmund's care. It's just so wrong – I know I would have done a good job had my father not changed everything – going to London to become a rich man and then losing it all. When I was a child I thought he was wonderful – I didn't know he was a fool. Damn him! Damn him!

Henry's heart was heavy as he walked back to his lodgings. Later, in front of a steaming meat pie, he pushed Edmund out of his mind. The pie was good. He picked up his tankard but it was empty so he handed it to the serving girl. Her name was Mary-Ann Simms and she was new but Henry had not really noticed her. She did her work well enough for Maria, Henry's landlady, to be satisfied – but her face was blank: it was as if she was somewhere else. She turned to walk over to the barrel with Henry's tankard and sighed. Henry heard her and it resonated with the sound of his own heart. Now that he had become aware of her he found himself watching her as he supped his ale and she swept the floor. It took him a few days to break through her reserve but eventually they were having short conversations whilst Mary-Ann worked.

'New tankard of ale?' Henry asked, then added, 'Bess wouldn't play today.'

Mary-Ann smiled. 'And who's Bess?' she asked as she went off to fill the tankard.

'An old girl. Wheezes a lot when she eats,' Henry answered as she returned, 'but not when her fire goes out.' He chuckled into his ale.

'You're talkin' in riddles.' She went off to see to another customer.

'Bess?' she quizzed as she came past a while later with her broom.

'A steam engine,' he explained a while later on his way back in from the privy. 'She's not really old. Quite new in fact. But difficult to control – sometimes the steam suddenly goes high and I have to release the safety valve – but then there's no power. They have to use the old hand tools for a bit 'til I get her up to steam again. Certainly appreciate me then!'

Mary-Ann laughed. 'Well you should have seen what we had in today.' Then she caught sight of the landlady watching her. 'Tell you later. Must do the mopping up.' Maria was standing next to the shelf upon which stood her barrels of ale and cider.

Henry approached her. 'Maria, when she's finished her tasks could she come and sit for a while with me?' He nodded in Mary-Ann's direction.

'Yes,' she replied although she looked at him in a way that reminded Henry of a schoolteacher.

He laughed. 'Just friendship.'

Maria smiled. 'Certainly, you could both do with some of that.'

3

After Mary-Ann had finished the landlady said something to her and pointed in Henry's direction. She came over to him, blushing slightly.

'She says I'm t'keep this customer happy. I wondered what on earth she meant for a moment until she pointed t'you,' she said, laughing.

'What did you have in earlier then?' he asked as she sat down.

'One of the old merchants from down on South Quay. Apparently he used t'live here in his youth. The doctors have told him he'll die soon so he wanted t'come back one last time.'

'And?'

'I've never seen anyone like him. He was enormous. He couldn't walk.'

'What, fat you mean?'

She nodded. 'Six servants carried him in on a board. He'd have been too fat to fit in a chair.'

Henry's eyebrows went up. 'Six! Rich man then. But he'd have to be to have had that much food.'

'You should have seen him. He was so fat that his whole body quivered like a jelly!' They both laughed and that evening they became friends. Henry found that he enjoyed her company. He wondered about her, about where she came from, but she was only a servant girl. She was far below the position of other young ladies whom his eyes had lighted upon – but she warmed his heart. His mind was logical and he knew the advantages a good marriage would confer: a rise in status would offset the disadvantage in which his father had left him. He liked Mary-Ann but he was determined that she would remain nothing more than a friend.

Most of the flour mills in the Yarmouth area were individually owned. The exception to this were the two mills at the bottom of St Nicholas Road: both belonged to the Flowers family. During that summer the miller had had problems with one of the smaller cogs that was part of the pulley system whereby he could move heavy sacks of grain or flour around the mill without having to support their weight. The second time Henry was there Mr Flowers was accompanied by a young woman.

'My daughter, Gloria,' Mr Flowers explained, and Henry took her hand and smiled. She smiled back, showing a gap in her front teeth. Henry was struck by the size and shape of her nose which looked as if it should belong to a brawling docker on South Quay.

'It's a pleasure to meet you,' he said. He was careful to keep his reactions from appearing on his face: Mr Flowers only had one child. Henry climbed the steps to the higher floors of the mill, leaving father and daughter behind. He had decided that the pulley wheel needed to be replaced and was just about to fit the hollow square end of his nut driver over the end of the bolt which attached the housing of the pulley to one of the beams when there was a loud shriek. He startled and moved towards the steps before he realised that the shriek had become a screeching laugh. It was Gloria and during the time he refitted the pulley she shrieked and laughed again. Later, walking back to the yard, he allowed himself a chuckle. Mr Flowers would have concerns about finding her a husband.

The following week Henry was working at the yard with his two apprentices, Jim and Freddie. The door to the yard opened and a young boy walked in. Henry went over to find out what his business was with them and as he approached he noticed that the boy's hair was flecked with white.

'Have you come from Boulters the bakers?' Henry asked him. 'It is too early for our order.' Spandlers had an arrangement with Boulters for bread at midday but the boy was shaking his head.

'I come from Mr Flowers. He wants you to check a pulley from the other mill.' Henry smiled to himself.

'I'll come later. At about two o' the clock,' he replied. The boy left and Henry turned to Jim and Freddie, James' sons. Henry was the millwright in charge of their apprenticeship.

'If Robert or your father is looking for me later when you're doing the iron moulding, I'll be at Flowers' mills.'

That afternoon, when Henry arrived at the mill, he found only the miller there and he said he was not staying while Henry worked because he had things he needed to do at the other mill. Henry frowned as he climbed the steps and wondered whether he had misinterpreted the situation. However, he had finished and was picking up his tools when he could hear voices. He had begun his descent of the steps when there was a shriek followed by laughter. He could not see through the floors of the mill but he thought he could hear another female voice. When he reached the ground floor the miller was there and behind him were the miller's wife and Gloria who was carrying a basket. As he approached she looked from one to the other of her parents. Her father nodded and she drew back a cloth that was covering the basket. Immediately there was a smell of ginger and other spices. Henry smiled at her.

'Norfolk gingers sir. Would you like one?' Henry smiled again and took a biscuit from the basket, aware as he did so that both her parents were observing him closely.

'These are delicious,' he said as he swallowed and both the women beamed at him. Gloria's ugliness was offset by the delight in her eyes although the sight of her mouth made Henry wonder why they had not trained her to keep her mouth closed when she smiled.

'Mr Spandler,' Mr Flowers cleared his throat. 'Mr Spandler, my daughter will be two and twenty next week. She has asked me if you could come and share a meal with us in our home.'

'It would be my pleasure,' Henry replied. He was careful to keep his satisfaction hidden. 'When would that be?'

6

'Friday next,' Mr Flowers replied, 'at six and half past, if that is possible. I do not know at what time you finish at Spandler's.'

Henry nodded and shook his hand before taking his cap from his jacket pocket. He turned to the two women and smiled.

'I will be there but I must return to the yard now,' he replied as he put his cap on, picked up his tools and left the mill.

Friday arrived and Henry arranged to leave the yard early. He wanted to have plenty of time to prepare himself to make an impression. Although he considered that Gloria was unattractive as a woman, she was the miller's only child, and that would be to his advantage if she became his wife. He asked Maria to have fresh clothes and hot water ready as he came in so that at half past six precisely he would be knocking at the door of the miller's home. Although the house was only one in a small terrace, when Henry entered he saw how comfortable they were and assumed that they had not moved to something grander because of the proximity of the mills. During the meal Henry tried to make conversation with Gloria: he wondered whether she would be better if her father was not there because he wouldn't let her say more than a few words before he interrupted and spoke for her. At least she managed to keep her screeching laugh under control while they ate. After the meal Mr Flowers suggested they left the ladies to their tea and he took Henry through to their lounge.

'I keep this for special occasions,' he said as he poured two glasses of whisky. Henry did not like spirits but he accepted it graciously. They sat down.

'Your business is doing well then?' asked Henry.

'You can tell?'

Henry laughed. 'Yes, we can always tell when a business is in difficulties because they try and fix the small problems themselves. You call us out for the smallest thing and we are glad to come.'

It was Mr Flowers' turn to laugh. 'So that your business will be profiting as well!'

Henry nodded. 'We are expanding and training more apprentices. We have to plan that some of us are working out of the yard each day because there's not really room otherwise.'

'It is not your generation that are running it yet though?'

'No but some of us are now fully trained and work alongside my uncles.'

'Your uncles? What of your father?' Henry suddenly realised that he had made a mistake.

'My father is dead.'

Mr Flowers beamed. 'So you will have inherited his share – you are already a man of means.' He paused when he saw the sudden pallor in Henry's face. 'You are aren't you?' His voice was anxious.

'I have to tell you, sir, that my father lost his share of the mill before he died.'

'Then you have no substance?'

'I am a millwright and skilled at my craft. My uncles pay me well.'

'Well enough to look after my daughter in the way she has come to expect? I do not think so. I am disappointed. You must leave us now.' Henry saw that he would be wasting his time to talk to this man. He stood and allowed Mr Flowers to show him the door.

2

As Henry and Mary-Ann became comfortable in each other's company, his heart began to smother the voice of logic – or at least to set it upon a different course. Although the miller's daughter had been unattractive to look upon, her father rejected him as a suitor. Gloria Flowers had appeared ugly and foolish to Henry although he'd have accepted that for the advantages of having her as a wife. What drawbacks would there need to be to the daughter of a man of substance before the father would consider him suitable? Mary-Ann had become a friend and one fine Sunday in early summer Henry asked her if she would like to walk along the seafront for a while. They walked down to the shore through St Nicholas's churchyard. Here there was an open drain: it took the rubbish out of town from the slaughterhouses and the Shambles area where butchers worked and usually it ran red. It was the same drain that, further along its length, flowed past the cottage in Garrison Walk where Henry had lived as a child and where he had had the responsibility of raising his father's family. The weather had been very hot and dry so that now the drain was full of stinking mud. In Mary-Ann's life bad smells were normal, but she wrinkled her nose that afternoon.

'Mary-Ann come away, that's horrible,' Henry said, a solicitous hand on her elbow. She nodded, moving away from the ditch.

'You'd think the town could do something about it.'

'Mmm, yes, but those who could don't ever see this. They live down by South Quay and come into church through the south gate.'

Mary-Ann had edged closer again, fascinated in spite of the smell. 'Look at that long fat tube in there. Looks like a sausage.' Just at that moment, the cow's intestine, inflated by the gases from the putrefying matter inside, split. They both gagged and broke into a run, their eyes watering. They were laughing as they came towards the gate that led from the churchyard onto the Denes. They looked at each other, their eyes met and time locked them in, momentarily: it was enough for their spirits to embrace but they did not touch. They both gasped and laughed, an unaccustomed gaiety making them feel airborne during the last few steps to the gate. As they came out onto the street they slowed to a walk: now they were two responsible young people taking a stroll.

In the months that followed they deliberately looked into each other's eyes many times when Mary-Ann was serving. Their times alone together were limited to Sunday afternoons when they walked amongst the fishermen's nets on the Denes or ventured down to the sands where small fishing boats, like beached whales, waited for the next tide. One afternoon they were leaning against the hull of one of those boats. The shore was quite busy and they were watching a family who were positioned nearby: the mother was sitting on an upright chair reading a newspaper whilst a servant girl held a parasol to shield her face from the sun and the father, dressed in a dark suit and hat, was showing a small boy how to crenellate the walls of his sandcastle. After a few moments Henry, caught unawares by the ball of emotion in his throat, looked away.

'Nice t'see a father playing with his child,' commented Mary-Ann. Henry, unable to trust his voice, nodded. Mary-Ann continued, 'I think all fathers ought t'play with their children, don't you?'

For a few minutes Henry didn't reply.

Then he spluttered, 'There's more to fatherhood than playing.' Suddenly aware that there was a problem, Mary-Ann looked at him, but then had the wisdom to look away and remain quiet. After a few minutes Henry started to talk. He told her how his father had sold his share of the yard and then returned from London crippled and penniless so that he had had to take on the responsibility of his father's family. As he told the story he struggled to control his emotions, especially when he spoke about his mother. Mary-Ann was overtaken by a strong desire to care for him. At the end of his story he said something that made her shiver. He was talking about his father.

'I raised his family. I will never support another man's children again. Even if in the future one of my brothers or sisters died, someone else would have to care for their children. I could not, I will not do it.' Although Henry was talking quietly his voice was hard, his eyes were wide open, bright with barely-controlled tears and his cheeks were flushed: to Mary-Ann it was as if he was shouting. She struggled to speak normally.

'I understand now why you are so sad sometimes.'

Henry nodded. 'Yes, but what about you? You rarely smile. I'm sure I'm not the only one with a secret.'

'I don't know what t'say.'

'You could just tell me.'

'I can't. I want us t'be friends. My mother advised me t'leave it at home. That no man would be want t'know me if he knew.' Mary-Ann was choosing her words carefully.

Henry looked at her. 'Have I made it worse by what I have just told you?' Mary-Ann's heart jumped. She nodded and looked at him but then quickly looked away: he was observing her closely.

'I... I,' she stammered, 'I have a child.'

'Tell me.' His voice was soft now.

'The farmer's son found me on my own one day and took me. You know?' She glanced at him and Henry nodded. 'I didn't want him to, but he said if I didn't let him he would get his father to evict us from the cottage and my father would lose his job. My parents wouldn't let me keep my b-baby because they said that it would cause trouble with the f-farmer.' She stopped and held her tongue between her teeth with enough pressure to cause pain, hoping it would give her some control over the tears which threatened. 'S-She went t'one of my father's cousins. They decided it would be best for me t'go away. That's when I came t'Yarmouth. S-She would be about two now. Probably doesn't know I'm her m-mother.' She gave in to the tears.

'And I've just said –.'

Mary-Ann sniffed and drew a deep breath. 'My mother said t'leave her in the past. "Start afresh, marry and have other children," she told me.' She paused to wipe the tears from her face. 'I've tried but I can still see her face. I cannot forget.' Henry looked down at his feet as she continued, 'and now I've told you.' At that she stopped and shook her head sadly.

For several moments only silence had a voice. Then Henry moved. He slid his hand across the hull of the boat and placed it on top of hers. A few moments later, still looking at the ground, he started to speak.

'I said I would never support another man's children. But she is your child. I'm fond of you. More than that I think I love you.' He looked at her but she was looking at the family next to them where the parents were talking and the child was removing the crenellations with the edge of his spade. 'Mary-Ann,' at the sound of her name she turned. He paused. She felt his hand. 'Mary-Ann.' His voice was firmer. 'I want to care for you – and your child.' Mary-Ann drew a sudden deep breath, but he continued. 'I can't marry you yet, but I will just as soon as I've saved the church fees. Will you trust me?'

Mary-Ann nodded and smiled, shaking the tears out of her eyes.

By this time the sun had gone down behind the rise in the town known as Fuller's Hill, signalling the end of Mary-Ann's time off. They walked back and for the first time she took his arm. As they made their way back up towards St Nicholas's church Henry smiled. It was a long time since he'd done that from a sense of happiness.

They turned right into North Road and saw Robert come out of the door to the yard. He was crossing the road towards Rampart Row when he looked back over his shoulder and saw them. Immediately he stopped, turned and came towards them. Henry could see that he was flustered.

'It's your Tom,' he said as he approached them. 'He's gone.' Henry froze with his mouth open. He felt Mary-Ann's grip tighten on his arm and shook himself.

'Gone! What do you mean?'

'He's left. There was a note on his bed. Says he's making his own way in the world.'

'What? Why?' Henry began to shake. 'W-Where's he gone?'

'I don't know. I'm sorry Henry.' Robert's eyes scanned his nephew's face and he frowned. 'The note didn't explain and no-one seems to know anything.'

'What about Edmund? Have you asked him?' Henry closed his mouth firmly before he said any more.

'Why do you think Edmund would know? It's true I know they weren't the best of friends.'

Henry shrugged. 'Tom once said to me that he was discontented – and he suggested Ed was the cause.' He sighed. 'I felt so happy a few moments ago. Mary-Ann has agreed to be my wife and I was coming to tell you we are going to set up home together.'

'That's wonderful news Henry. I'm glad that you've found someone to make you happy. I'm sure Tom will come back soon.'

'Yes,' Henry retorted, 'perhaps as soon as he finds he cannot earn enough to fill his belly.' He attempted a smile but it became a grimace. 'Ask Edmund though, he may know something,' he added.

'Henry,' Mary-Ann put her other hand on his shoulder, 'I have t'go. Maria will be cross.'

'James and I are going to ask at some of the taverns to see if anyone has seen him,' said Robert. 'We're meeting at the Angel in about half an hour.' Henry nodded and he and Mary-Ann turned from Robert and walked towards Rampart Row.

Later, when Henry arrived at the Angel Inn, there was a large group gathered including his uncles and men from the yard. Edmund was there. Henry met his eyes.

'I'm s-sorry he's g-gone,' stuttered Edmund. 'I spoke harshly to him last night. I didn't think he'd go away.'

'Why? Is it because you've done it before and he's just been upset but not done anything?' Henry glared at Edmund who looked down at the floor.

'We'll find him.' Edmund raised his head again and Henry could see the panic in his eyes. 'We'll find him,' Edmund repeated, 'and when we do I promise you that he will find I have changed.' Henry looked into his eyes, nodded and turned from him to see his uncles looking at him. He did not approach them: anger made him unsure of his speech.

Tom was on a boat on his way up the river to Norwich, working his passage by rowing. He was part of a team of six and by the time they arrived his hands were raw and it was dark. He spent that night under the upturned boat and the following day found work as a porter at the railway station. After a day's work his overseer took him to a house near the station and recommended him to the family there who allowed him to sleep in a corner of the attic. In Yarmouth, over the next few days, Robert had posters printed with his description and these were placed all over the town. Tom would have been astonished at his uncle's efforts to find him. After a week Henry pondered whether he would ever hear of Tom again: he was one of his father's children whom he'd been given charge of nine years ago. He despaired but could only hope that he was still alive. Tom's disappearance reawakened the guilt that he felt because of his siblings who had died and Henry drank more of Maria's ale than he usually did.

Whenever Mary-Ann Simms looked at him he was frowning. 'He is your father's child,' she said to him one evening.

'But he is gone,' he replied without looking at her.

'Let him go. He has made a man's decision for himself. He is no longer your responsibility. I used t'check my baby's blanket was tucked around her before I went t'sleep and when she went I would worry that she was cold. Then I would think that they weren't feeding her properly. I came to realise that I can't help her.' She put a hand on his arm but quickly withdrew it when she saw Maria looking at them. 'I know it makes you sad but you can do nothing for Tom now.'

Henry looked up. 'You understand like no-one else. At this moment I want to take you into my arms but Maria would have apoplexy.' Mary-Ann chuckled which made Henry's face light up and he smiled. 'On the morrow I will see one of my uncles and tell him I want to set up home with you. Perhaps he will help us.'

Five weeks later Henry and Mary-Ann moved into rooms in a row of houses called Francis Buildings next to the new workhouse on North Road. The door to their dwelling opened directly from the road into a passage from which climbed a steep, narrow staircase where another family lived. With Robert's help they were able to afford the two downstairs rooms: the door to the first was in the passage to the left of the front door and had an opening in one of the walls which led through to the room behind. At the end of the passage there was a door which led to the yard where there was a privy which they shared with the family upstairs. Robert and James were with them the day they moved in and they arrived carrying a table which James had crafted for them.

'Well think of it, James,' said Robert, 'young Henry in his own home.' They put the new table down in the living room. Henry moved his hand over the surface, feeling the surface.

'Thank-you indeed – for everything,' said Henry, while Mary-Ann blushed and hung onto his arm. James put a hand on his shoulder.

'I'm sure you'll better yourself beyond this,' he said. Henry laughed and his eyes met Mary-Ann's.

'We're quite happy where we are for now.'

'I think, James, that we should leave them,' said Robert.

'Before you go, we need to ask your advice.' said Henry, aware that Mary-Ann was suddenly gripping his arm tighter. 'There is a child.' Mary-Ann looked at the floor. 'She lives with a cousin of Mary-Ann but we would like her to come and live with us. Do you think we should?'

'Your family may object, Mary-Ann,' replied Robert gently, 'especially those that at present have the care of her but if you feel that you can do it, I will arrange with the King's Arms to have the horse and you can go and try to bring her here to your home.' While they had been speaking Mary-Ann had continued looking at the floor but now she looked up and met Robert's eyes.

'Th-Thank-you,' she stuttered. The two older men looked at each other and left. After the door shut behind them Henry swept Mary-Ann into his arms and held her tightly. His eyelids were tightly shut and his eyeballs moved rapidly behind them. After a few moments Mary-Ann pulled away, breathing rapidly.

'I could scarcely find my breath,' she laughed as her eyes danced. Henry met her eyes and his mouth smiled. She could not see his fingernails digging into his palms: under his roof, again, there would be a child for whom he had the ultimate responsibility.

Later, in the sleeping room, Henry's hands shook as he unhooked Mary-Ann's stays. He felt her body tense beneath his hands. She shivered as he moved the undergarment down under her arms. He realised her fear and turned her so she was facing him. Quiet tears were rolling down her face.

'Oh, Mary-Ann!' he exclaimed as he hugged her to himself. Her body felt stiff and unyielding in contrast to the soft gentleness he'd felt that afternoon. 'Are you frightened? I won't hurt you.' She nodded and sniffled.

'But it will hurt. I know. Did before.'

'Then we will not do it. We will lie, warm each other and sleep. You are not yet my wife.'

In bed they lay wrapped around each other and in the darkness Henry traced his finger over her face, feeling her nose and the line of her lips and working his way round to her ear where he fondled her ear lobe. He could feel her softening beneath his caresses and smiled to himself. He forced himself to lie still. He was sure that, in a short while, she would want him to do what his growing penis desired. Then he switched his thoughts to the following day when he would be out on a cold mill-cap with Jim and Freddie. They slept.

On the Friday of that week Robert called Henry into the office.

'You're not on duty tomorrow. I have arranged for you to use the horse. Pick it up from the King's Arms and use our cart to take Mary-Ann to find her child. I hope it works out well for you.'

Henry nodded. 'Thank-you. We appreciate all you have done for us.'

Robert laughed. 'You are a valuable part of this business and you're my nephew. On both counts I would see you happily settled.'

On the following morning Henry and Mary-Ann were on the road to Caister. The seat at the front of the cart was open and Henry was glad that the autumn rains had not yet started. The countryside was flat and wide and they chattered happily as they travelled.

After a few hours they reached her mother's house. Abigail Simms was standing on the doorstep and saw them coming.

'Mary-Ann! You're here. How did you know?' she asked.

'Know what?'

'There's problems with t'child. They want us to have her. George lost his job.'

'We've come to take her.'

'It's just as well because we really can't have her.'

'What would've happened if we hadn't come?'

'Workhouse.' Abigail shrugged. 'There's nothing else they could do. They can't feed their own and didn't know where you were. I'll fetch her. You stay here.'

'Ma, as soon as you bring her we'll go. I don't want her becoming upset because we're taking her.'

'I don't think she'll do that.' Abigail left and Mary-Ann looked around her childhood home. It was one of two farm-workers' cottages that leant against each other so that they propped each other up. There was a room downstairs in which the family lived and her parents slept and above was the room she'd shared with all her brothers and sisters. She looked up the stairs and there were cobwebs.

'They've not bothered to move their bed upstairs now that we've all gone. I suppose they've always slept down here.'

'I'm just going out to the privy,' said Henry. Mary-Ann sat down on the stool. She smiled to herself, remembering when all her older siblings had left and she'd finally been allowed to use it. Before that she'd always just sat on the floor. She looked through the door which Henry had left open and could see into the garden. She followed him out and started to rub the plants between her thumb and fingers, smelling her hands.

'What are those?' Henry asked.

'Ma's plants. They have lots of uses especially when you're ill.'

'Sounds as if she is one of the witches we learnt about in history at school.'

'I think sometimes the villagers used to gossip about her. But they are very quick to come looking for her help when they needed it.'

'Yes, they are,' said Abigail who had just returned, 'and you can take some of those back with you if you want.

The ones you know how to use that is.' Standing next to her holding her hand was a thin, bedraggled girl, who, when she realised Abigail had stopped walking, sat down and started rocking herself. Mary-Ann smiled at her but there was no response. Abigail passed Mary-Ann an old rag.

'Dip it in t'water-butt and wrap the plants you take in it. They'll stay fresher.'

On the way back to Yarmouth the little girl sat between them. She had not cried when they'd taken her and leaned against Mary-Ann as if she hadn't the strength to sit up.

'We still have some food left over,' said Henry. The little girl suddenly looked up, the first reaction she'd had. 'I think she's hungry – but be careful.'

Mary-Ann nodded. 'Yes, I don't want t'make her sick,' she replied as she felt down into her bag and took out some bread. She broke off a small piece and held it out towards the girl. Her eyes opened wide but she did not move.

'Bread – for you.' Mary-Ann smiled at the girl and held the piece up to her mouth. By the third piece the girl was looking from the bag to Mary-Ann.

'There's some cheese as well.' She held out a tiny bit and this time the girl reached out for it. She put it into her mouth and smiled at Mary-Ann. When she'd swallowed she leant forward and tried to look into Mary-Ann's bag. Mary-Ann reached in and brought out the water bottle which she unstopped. She held the lip of the bottle up to the girl's lips and she slurped the water.

'Thirsty as well little one?' Henry asked. At the sound of his deep voice the girl jumped and curled down towards Mary-Ann.

'Don't be frightened,' Mary-Ann said as she stroked her matted hair. 'I'm your Ma and this man will be your Pa now.' Henry was careful not to react, keeping his eyes on the road ahead; he gripped the reins tightly. Mary-Ann did not notice and continued, 'I did not name her when she was born.

I knew they were going t'take her away after the first few weeks so I made myself just call her baby.'

'What would you like to call her? Do you want her to be Mary-Ann whilst that is your name?

Mary-Ann shook her head. 'It hasn't been a fortunate name, I would not wish her t'have it. Louisa's pretty though and I had a friend called Louisa in the village. She did well for herself – wed the son of a cobbler.' The words had tumbled out of her.

'Then Louisa she will be,' declared Henry.

'Do you not want t'say a name yourself? Your t'be her father – is there not some other you would prefer?'

'When you have your next girl, who will be a child from my body, we will call her Caroline. I promised my sister.'

Mary-Ann squeezed his arm. 'She was the one who looked after your mother? Is that right?'

'It is,' replied Henry with a smile. This was why he liked Mary-Ann so much. She remembered and knew what was important to him.

Over the next few days Louisa started to play and make small sounds. She would not leave Mary-Ann's side, following her everywhere. She cried when Mary-Ann put her in the small bed that Henry had made which was in the corner of the room in which they slept but Mary-Ann refused to allow her to climb into their bed. The child was still wary of Henry, causing Mary-Ann to wonder whether her cousin's husband had ill-treated her. Mary-Ann loved her and watched everything she did: she was making up for the time she had lost with her daughter.

'I could go into Row five after I've finished at the yard. There's a family I know there who keep a cow and I could buy some milk for her,' suggested Henry.

Mary-Ann shook her head. 'My Ma always told us not t'trust the milk you could buy in the towns; told us it would do us no good.'

'Yes but this is fresh milk, doesn't have the sourness milk usually has because they have their own cow, just like on a farm.'

'No, not just like on a farm. Where's the field where the cow can eat green grass?' Henry laughed but she continued, 'I saw a farmer calling in at the new workhouse today. I think I'll go at the same time tomorrow and see if he will sell some t'me.'

The following day whilst Mary-Ann was at the door of the workhouse talking to the farmer a cart arrived. In the back was a young boy, bound hand and foot.

'It's the Norwich cart,' the farmer told her. Mary-Ann frowned and he explained, 'Those of Yarmouth who fall on hard times in Norwich are brought back here. Their own parish has t'feed them.'

'But why is he bound?'

'So that he cannot run off and try and find shelter at another workhouse although this one here is better than many others hereabouts, so they say.' Mary-Ann watched while the driver of the cart cut the binding on the boy's ankles. She winced when the driver pulled him from the cart and he stumbled but she saw that he was quite tall so perhaps not as young as she had first thought. The driver pulled a book from the pocket of his jacket, flicked through it until he found the page he wanted.

'Mark it here,' he said to the man at the workhouse door. 'Thomas Spandler.' Mary-Ann's hand flew to her mouth.

'Thomas Spandler did you say?' The men all turned to look at her and she became flustered. 'B-but that's the name of my man's brother! He's lost.'

'You'll have to fetch him then ma'am,' the man said.

Mary-Ann quickly returned to the house. She untied Louisa from the table leg where she'd put her whilst she went to fetch the milk. She wailed so Mary-Ann gave her a little of the milk and tied some more sugar in her rag. She had not taken off her own cloak. She hoisted Louisa onto her hip and left the house. She knew Henry had said that she must not disturb him at the yard but she was sure he would want to know what she had seen.

When she reached the yard, she pushed open the door from the street and walked down the passage which went under the second storey of the cottage. She drew a deep breath and peered around the corner of the building hoping to see Henry but he wasn't there. Robert, however, had seen her. He came to her and escorted her into the cottage, through the office and into the parlour.

'This is Henry's Mary-Ann,' he said to Mary his wife. He turned to Mary-Ann, 'This my wife Mary. Now this must be your child?'

Mary-Ann nodded. 'However, she is not the reason I have come calling. Where is Henry?'

'Out at a mill,' replied Robert, 'is something wrong?' he asked as Mary-Ann looked crestfallen.

'It's just that,' Mary-Ann took a deep breath, 'th-that I think I have seen Thomas.'

'Thomas! Where?'

'At the workhouse.' Mary-Ann described what she had seen.

'I will send for Henry.' Robert left the cottage and went out into the yard, leaving the two ladies together.

'I-I should be going home,' Mary-Ann stuttered. 'Henry said that he would arrange a time to bring me and introduce me.'

'You're here now and I would not let you depart without even a cup of tea.' Mary smiled at Mary-Ann who looked anxious. 'I will set it right with your Henry and, besides, I would meet you. Please sit down.' Louisa had gone to sleep on Mary-Ann's hip and was heavy and the invitation to sit overcame her anxiety.

'I have some ginger cake. Would you like some?' Mary asked.

'Yes please. You are very kind.' Mary-Ann looked around and, noticing the furnishings and being aware that Mary had sent a young girl to bring the tea and cake, she suddenly felt nervous again. The living standards of these people reminded her of the farmer for whom her father worked and she wondered whether she could ever fit into this family. Was Henry just with her because he could not find anyone better?

Later that afternoon she was back at the house in Francis Buildings. The door opened and in came Henry and Robert with the young boy whom she had seen being taken out of the cart.

'We've brought him out of the workhouse. He cannot stay there. He's a Spandler,' Henry explained. 'He doesn't want to go back to Robert's cottage so he is going to stay here.'

'I have an old mattress that he can use to sleep on. He would have to sleep in here.' Robert looked round the small room where Mary-Ann cooked and which was generally their living room. 'There's just about enough space in the corner there.' Mary-Ann's heart thumped in her chest. Her life was changing so quickly: only a few weeks ago she was a servant girl in a lodging house, now she was looking after a small family. Louisa, who had been asleep, woke up and cried. Mary-Ann smiled. She was unsure about this youth whom her Henry said was coming to live with them, but Louisa was her child.

In Norwich Tom had been cheated and wrongly accused of theft. Eventually, starving and destitute, he had taken himself to the workhouse. He had not realised they would take him back to Yarmouth and when Mary-Ann had recognised his name he had been overcome with shame. Henry mentioned working at the yard and to his surprise Tom readily agreed: the adventure had made him wiser. In the first few days Tom looked at the ground a lot. When he was handed a broom and told to sweep out the yard, as was the practice with all the new apprentices, Edmund had smirked but Tom had not noticed. When he reached the part of the yard where the lathes were and where most of the light, papery waste was, Edmund had deliberately moved to sit with his legs spread-eagled so as to make Tom's task more difficult, until he saw his father and Henry looking at him, when he quickly moved away. Tom had ignored him. Freddie and Jim, Henry's apprentices, befriended him and he was disappointed although not surprised when Robert said that he could not be Henry's apprentice. Robert said that he would take him on himself. After a few days at the yard, where he was learning new things and using his hands, he was glad he had been found.

A few days later, Rosa, the woman of the family upstairs, stopped Mary-Ann by the front door of the house they shared.

'You have another mouth to feed?' she asked.

Mary-Ann nodded. 'He's started work at the yard with Henry. He's his brother.'

'I've just been taken on by Gordon's on the market – my Jim's had his wages cut,' she explained in response to Mary-Ann's quizzical look. 'His boss said it was either that or find work somewhere else. I wondered – could you have my Susie when I'm out. I-I couldn't pay you much.'

'I suppose I would be at home anyway with Louisa. She's still settling in and regaining her strength and Henry's not said that I'll need t'earn some money.' Mary-Ann paused and glanced up the stairs. 'I've had an idea. Do you use the attic?'

'Two of the oldest children sleep there and Jim has his fishing things up there. Why?'

'Well young Tom is sleeping in the corner of our living area. I keep tripping over his mattress and I'd just started training Louisa t'stay in that corner when I'm cooking. If he could sleep in the attic – he wouldn't be able to afford a proper rent – but if I looked after Susie then from the little he earns he could pay both of us for lodging and food.'

'Then the children would have to squeeze together with us,' Rosa replied, 'but that's better than going hungry.'

Thus it was that Tom moved his bed up into the attic of the house.

That night, in their bed, Mary-Ann snuggled up to Henry. He caressed her, as he'd done each night since they'd moved into their own home. He traced his fingers over her face before moving his fingers down her neck until eventually he could feel the soft mound of her breast. She sighed.

'Are you alright?' he asked.

'Yes, I've been thinking. On the farm where I grew up I've seen the animals joining many times. It does not seem to hurt them. The other day, when we'd cuddled and afterwards I needed to use the bucket I noticed that I was very wet and sticky. Maybe that's my body's way of making it easier? It hurt before because the farmer's son just took me roughly before my body was ready. But it's not like that with you.' As she spoke Henry smiled in the darkness: his patience was about to have its reward. He slowly moved his hand up her leg, stopping when he felt her tense up and caressing her leg until she relaxed again. Eventually he reached her vulva. It was wet and she shivered with his touch.

'I think you're ready now,' he said, his voice unsteady with anticipation.

3

It was five months since Henry had set up home with Mary-Ann. At the end of his working day he left the yard and, forgetting where he was walking, turned down Rampart Row to Maria's lodging house. He realised what he had done when he was approaching the front door and stopped. Instantly he had a fierce longing to be in there, supping ale, free from any responsibilities and on his own: his new family felt like a heavy weight. He knew Maria would not welcome him because when Mary-Ann had told her that they were moving into Francis Buildings together she'd told them it was improper and they should wait until they had saved the church fees for the marriage. He turned around and walked back up the row with his fists curled into balls, looking at no-one. A crushing sadness overwhelmed him: Mary-Ann, he thought, loved him and he knew his younger brother, Tom, looked up to him – but he felt worthless. As he walked a logical part of his brain asked him why he was suddenly thinking like this: he'd been fine as he left the yard. He had no answer. At the top of the Row he did not turn left to go to Francis Buildings but instead turned right and stepped inside the Plough. Usually he would go to the King's Arms if he wanted a drink but his uncles or cousins might be in there and he wanted to be on his own.

He drank his first tankard, and most of his second, quite quickly. He wanted the ale, partly because he was thirsty having helped to prepare a new tree trunk for the lathe that afternoon, but also because he had made himself feel better that way before. As he started his third a picture of his home, with Mary-Ann, appeared in his mind. He could see her cooking over the open fire with Louisa playing in the corner whilst she chatted to Tom. She wouldn't be wondering where he was yet because sometimes he would spend time with his uncles at the end of the day especially if there were projects at the yard that needed talking through. In his imagination he felt her smallness and fragility as he put his arms round her. He doubted himself but he loved her, felt the urge to be her protector and wanted to be with her. His third tankard was still half full when he left the Plough.

At home the first thing he did was to sweep Mary-Ann into his arms, making her giggle. As he clung onto her and gripped her more closely she stopped laughing and pulled herself away. He let her go. She looked at him and her grey eyes, warm with concern, flicked over his face. She frowned although she did not ask him what was wrong.

'Go and have your wash. Tom's filled the water bucket. Food will be ready soon.'

Henry nodded and smiled. The darkness had lifted as suddenly as it had descended.

As they lay in bed that night Henry shared with Mary-Ann what had happened after work and how he'd felt.

'Thank God you came back to us. We need you. I was just a serving maid and you've made me happy. Th-the thought of you not being here makes me want to cry.'

'No, don't do that. I just felt as if I was of no use, that you'd be better off without me. I'm not good enough for you.'

'What do you mean? When I had tea with Mary at the cottage after I'd told Robert about Tom I felt then that your family was above me – that if you could find someone better you'd leave me.'

'I tried to find the hand of others who were better off than you, it is true.' His arm was around Mary-Ann and he felt her sudden tension. 'No, not now, it couldn't happen now even if those pompous fathers came and begged me to take their daughters!' He chuckled and she relaxed. 'That was before I really knew you, before I'd fallen in love with you and discovered how lovely you are. I thought I needed to marry into a family that could offset the disadvantage my father left me in, but I do not care about that now.' Henry stopped and

27

chewed his lip. 'Earlier tonight I thought I was a failure. I-I thought that I wouldn't be able to look after you properly.'

'But you do! Don't you see? I'm in my home, not someone's serving maid and I have my Louisa with me.' It was her turn to laugh. 'I know you love me – you've been so gentle when most men would have been rough and demanding. Besides your family has more money than mine and I don't think they accept me. Mary looked at me curiously when I spoke. I think she thinks I'm just a country girl. Since then I've been trying to change the way I speak.'

Henry hugged her closely. 'I had noticed. You're clever enough to see what you need to do to fit in. I don't care what Mary thinks, or Robert, or any of the family. Soon they'll forget where you're from and even if they don't you're more than good enough for me – if they don't like it they will just have to get used to it.'

'And you're doubting yourself because of all that happened with your family after your father left.' Mary-Ann squeezed him. 'You were unfortunate for that to happen to you. It doesn't make you incapable, it just means that you have the experience to take us through any difficulties that may be ours in time to come. I think we should be together. It was meant to be.'

'You're right. The past was horrible and it makes me sad, but we're together now.' In the darkness Henry smiled.

It was their spirits, not their bodies, that had coupled that night.

The next day, as usual, Henry and Tom walked from their home in Francis Buildings, along North Road, to the yard. Henry greeted townsfolk whom he knew; he walked tall and straight; his arms hung by his side with hands relaxed, not curled into fists, and he was excited by his life. He remembered the evening before and wondered at himself: how foolish he was because today he could do anything he wanted!

He was so energised that he was impatient to arrive at the yard and start work.

Henry was proud at the way Tom had put his troubles behind him and had settled down to work at the yard. He thought of his father and remembered his pride when he himself had started: Henry had a sense of satisfaction because Tom was doing what his father would have wanted. The strong young man walking alongside him was there because of decisions Henry had made and he knew that if his father had been alive and was the man Henry remembered before he'd lost his mind seeking his fortune in London, he would be proud. They chatted as they walked, mostly about the yard and the work they were doing, and they enjoyed each other's company.

'I like being taught by Uncle Robert,' said Tom. 'I wasn't very sure at first. He'd always seemed so abrupt at the cottage when I lived there that I didn't think he'd be very good at explaining. He was telling me how stirring the molten iron changes it and he made it easy to understand. Today we are going to do several test pieces so that I can see how they're different. It's interesting.'

Henry nodded. 'And what about you? Have you recovered? You seem to have put some weight on.'

'Yes, I think I have. I still feel weak though sometimes. Yesterday we were moving the new stock of pig iron from the delivery wagon into the storage room and I fell as I put a load on the floor. The room moved as I bent down!' Tom laughed. 'Uncle Robert made me sit down for a while and Aunt Mary brought me a drink. Edmund didn't like that and he scowled at me.'

'How's it been with Edmund?'

Tom shrugged. 'He's like a pesky fly. Tries to annoy me but I just ignore him. He's not worth taking any notice of.'

'Probably the best way of dealing with him.'

'Like I said, he's just a nuisance. If I think of some of the men I had to deal with in Norwich...' Tom's voice trailed off just as they arrived at the yard and could hear Robert talking.

'They've said the line should be open in about two years.' Robert, unusually, was standing with the men who were warming themselves by Bessie, the yard's stationary steam engine and the adjoining furnace where the iron moulding took place. He turned to face Henry and Tom when he saw several of the men look in their direction as they came around the corner of the alley.

'We wondered whether you two were coming to work today,' James, Robert's brother, called. Everyone laughed and Henry looked flustered until he came nearer and saw the merriment on James's face.

'I've some news.' Robert's deep voice cut across the laughter. 'The railway's coming to Yarmouth!'

'Moving steam engines!' Henry's voice squeaked with excitement.

'Trust him to think about the engines first,' James said and they all laughed again. Everyone knew and appreciated Henry's skill at running Bessie.

'I was at a meeting and they told us that they have to raise an enormous amount of money,' explained Robert. 'Apparently that's the difficult part and will take quite a long time. Then once the work starts we will soon have a railway.'

'To London?'

'No, Norwich. They started a line from London years ago but ran out of money when they were about half way here. This will not be as long and will be easier to build.'

'It will change the town,' stated James.

Henry frowned. 'Will it be better for us? We will be able to reach the mills and pumps near Norwich more easily but then I suppose the millwrights in Norwich may come here and take our business.'

'That's as it may be,' James replied, 'but I think it's in the summer months that we will see a difference. People pass comment now on the number of visitors but there will be many more when they can come on the train.'

'Where will the station be?'

'That's yet to be decided,' said Robert, 'but it will need to be over the river somewhere unless they're going to pull down much of the town.' He looked around his men. 'It will be a new time for us all – but for now we have work to do.' The group around the steam engine moved away, some to the lathes or the huge workbenches and others left the yard to go out to mills or pumps in the area. Henry turned to Bessie.

'She's coming up to steam,' said Freddie. 'Fire from the main furnace hadn't been pushed into the connecting chamber when we arrived.'

'But we thought you would want it moving into our side,' added Jim, 'and we've built it up and now it's burning well.' Jim and Freddie, sons of James, Robert's brother, were Henry's apprentices. Henry nodded his approval.

'When it's up to pressure we'll set the belts running so they can use the tools. Meanwhile you can continue with the chisel work on that trunk we had on the lathe yesterday. Then when Bessie's stabilised we're spending the rest of the morning in the work-room. We're learning about sails and how we use the wind.' The work-room had a black-board and desks and it was where the apprentices learnt the theory of their craft: Jim and Freddie groaned.

At the end of the working day Henry returned home. As he opened the door from the passage he heard Louisa laugh.

'Pa!' Her smile as he came through the door made his heart jump. He went towards her but she retreated behind Mary-Ann's skirts.

'She called me Pa!' Mary-Ann stirred the pot that was on the fire, moved it to one side, away from the strongest part of the fire, and put the lid on. She picked up Louisa and sat down on one of the benches which ran down either side of the table. Henry frowned in puzzlement: she would usually sit in one of the chairs when she cuddled Louisa because the arms of the chair gave her some support.

'Come and sit with me for a while. The food will not spoil for a bit more cooking.' Henry sat down next to her and immediately Louisa wriggled round to sit on the knee furthest away from him. Henry put his arm round Mary-Ann leaning her towards him but Louisa cowered back under her arm. She was only a small child and Mary-Ann's arm reached around her and rested on her own lap. Henry placed his free hand on top of hers; they looked at each other and smiled.

'What have you been doing today at the yard? You don't seem to have been working hard?'

Henry chuckled. 'You mean I'm not sweaty and covered with sawdust? No, we've spent most of the day in the work-room doing theory. It's surprising how tired I feel even though I've done no real work. But I've some news. I almost forgot. Robert told us this morning that the railway is coming to Yarmouth – you'll be able to go to Norwich on the train, do your shopping and come back all in the same day!'

'Sounds exciting but I don't understand why – we have shops in Yarmouth!'

While they were speaking Louisa had been looking from one to the other of them. She saw the smiles on their faces and, although she did not understand what they were talking about, she sensed they were happy. She watched their hands, joined together on Mary-Ann's lap, and saw Henry stroking Mary-Ann with his finger. Her small hand moved forward, whilst her eyes kept darting between their faces and their hands; she placed it on top of Mary-Ann's. They both smiled at her. Henry kept stroking Mary-Ann and as he did he reached out with his finger so that he touched Louisa with each stroke. Louisa smiled at him and moved forward out from under Mary-Ann's arm. Slowly, gently, Henry moved his hand until it was encompassing both of them. He wanted to laugh, loudly, but he stopped himself lest he frightened her.

Tom came in. Mary-Ann lifted Louisa from her knee and returned to her cooking. She stirred the mixed potatoes, carrots and swede and reached up for her frying pan from its hook on the wall. Earlier that day she had been on the market and bought a lump of bacon. This she diced and, when the pan was hot she added it together with a chopped-up onion. By the time both men had washed there were tasty smells and sizzling sounds.

'This is going to be good, Mary-Ann,' declared Tom as he sat down on the bench and Henry sat next to him. From her corner Louisa watched the two men. Other evenings she had stayed in her corner until Mary-Ann put the food on the plates and came and picked her up. This night she toddled over to the other side of the table and climbed up. She did not make eye contact with either of the two men but instead focussed on what Mary-Ann was doing.

Henry rolled from on top of Mary-Ann and lay panting for a few moments. Mary-Ann snuggled up next to him and soon his breathing became regular. She lay, her eyes open, rubbing her hand over her belly and her movement broke the light sleep into which Henry had fallen.

'Are you alright? I was rough tonight.'

'Yes, but you made me become wet first so it didn't hurt.' Mary-Ann paused. 'Henry I-I nearly told you when we were sitting on the bench with Louisa only I wasn't sure. The smell of the fat frying made me feel sickly. I remember it well.'

Henry sat up. 'What? Are you ill?'

'No,' Mary-Ann chuckled, 'I'm with child. I thought I might be because I should have had my bleeding last week and it didn't come. Then, tonight, feeling sick made me sure.'

Henry lay down again and turned to face her. He reached out and touched her face.

'Are you sure you're alright? I would have been gentler if I had known.' Mary-Ann laughed. 'You don't need

33

to worry about that. My mother sat on me and bounced up and down to try and dislodge Louisa. It hurt but it didn't work. Then she gave me a horrible drink she'd made from one of her herbs and sent me to my bed with a stick. She told me to use it on myself to poke out the baby. I tried it once; it made me bleed and I was frightened so I stopped. I don't think anything you could do, big though you are, would move the babe.' Henry moved his hand to her stomach and caressed it.

'My child is in here. My child,' he repeated as he hugged her closely.

Later that night Henry woke, sweating profusely. All that he remembered from his nightmare was of Mary-Ann sitting up in a coffin. She was holding a bloody stick.

4

A week later, at the yard, Robert called Henry in to see him.

'I'm concerned that my favourite nephew seems to be carrying the sort of frown that I thought you'd lost when you found Mary-Ann.' Henry looked at Robert but remained silent. 'I feel there is something troubling you. Is it Tom?'

Henry shook his head. 'No, not Tom,' he hesitated but then continued, 'I'm having nightmares again. Like I used to when my siblings kept dying.' He shuddered. 'You see, Mary-Ann is with child and I'm worried that the same thing will happen, that the child will die, or Mary-Ann, or both. I couldn't stop it then and I feel I have to protect them now but I cannot think of anything I can do. But I must stop it!' Henry's voice had risen in pitch and volume.

'Does Mary-Ann know?' Henry shook his head.

'I've had the nightmare three times in this last week,' Henry paused and drew breath, 'but each time I've managed to wake quietly. I'm worried that I will disturb Mary-Ann and that I'll frighten her.

'You would be better to tell her calmly when you are both awake than for her to find out suddenly in the middle of the night when she is half asleep.'

'Yes, I've been thinking that myself. I think I would feel better if she knew. But then again I wonder if it would perturb her to realise how affected I am.'

'I think you'll find your Mary-Ann to be stronger than you imagine. My Mary was very taken with her. Said she was intelligent – timid at first but answered well.'

A fleeting smile crossed Henry's face. 'Yes, you know I'd told her not to disturb me when I was at work? But she realised how important it was, seeing Tom...'

'It must have taken some courage to come here that morning,' Robert interrupted, 'to a yard full of men she didn't know.'

'Your Mary was here.'

'Yes, but she'd never met her and, besides, would she have known she was here before she set off?' Henry shook his head.

'You're right. I will tell her tonight.' Henry paused. 'You think I can, don't you?'

'What – tell Mary-Ann?' The tone of Robert's voice expressed his amazement.

'No, be a man with my own family.' Henry swallowed several times. 'Th-the others, m-my siblings…'

'That was no fault of yours. Look what you have done. More than any man should expect his son to do. My older brother, your father, it was he that failed his family. The fact that any of you survived, and that those that have are taking their places in the world, is testament to you. William was a fine young man and was becoming an excellent millwright when he died – a tragic accident. Eliza and Mary have both turned into lovely young women. Rachel is turning out the same and Martha is a strong, happy little girl. As for Tom, well I'm so glad he is back. I can tell already that he is going to be as big an asset to this business as his older brother.' Henry held onto Robert's desk for support because he felt his legs become wobbly beneath him. 'Here, sit down young man,' continued Robert, 'you are clearly not well.' He rang his bell and when the servant girl appeared he asked for tea and cake for both of them. 'I will sup with you. We need to spend some time together, you and I.'

Later that day, when Henry shared with Mary-Ann, she was shocked, never having realised the extent to which his past had hurt him. She cried with him when he cried.

The months flew by and by spring Henry could see his baby deforming Mary-Ann's stomach. The time he'd spent sharing with Robert and later with Mary-Ann had stopped the nightmares. Now all he felt was a child-like anticipation for the baby which caused him to occasionally leap into the air as he walked along, much to the amusement of Tom.

In St Nicholas's church, at Easter, Mary-Ann took her place next to Henry in the Spandler pews. Her face showed her awe at being inside this huge place of worship: her village church would fit inside St Nicholas's many times.

'Henry, do you think Robert would let us use the cart again?' she asked him after the service. They were standing in the yard near the cottage. A rope had been tied, keeping the family away from the working part of the yard where the furnace was still hot and there were sharp and dangerous tools. The children were allowed to play. Mary, Robert's wife, had provided them all with a meal of bread and cold meats and cheese.

'Why? Do you have a sudden desire to see your parents?' Henry answered.

Mary-Ann nodded. 'My mother particularly – I want her to come and help me when I labour. She has come to the aid of many of the women in the village. They only call for her if things go wrong but I want her here all the time. I think the baby will come early in July but I can't be sure. It's not the best time for the farm – that would be in the middle of winter – but at least it's not later when the main harvest is due. But for now I'd like to go and visit, perhaps even stay for a few days. I'd like to learn more about her herbs. She showed me some as I was growing up but I wasn't so interested then. Now that I have my own family I would like to know some more.'

'You'll need to write and ask when you can come,' suggested Henry. Mary-Ann looked surprised and then laughed.

'I cannot write but even if I could they wouldn't be able to read it.'

'What, not even your Pa?'

'My Pa spent his young years as a bird-scarer in the fields.' Mary-Ann shrugged. 'That is the difference between my family and yours. Do you know that is the first time I've been to a church service and sat in a pew? Always stood at the back before.'

'Yes, but that does not make us better than you. Look at Edmund. He has all the advantages of money and position, but he is lazy and mean to those less fortunate than himself. You are worth many Edmunds. I will ask Robert – but for now come and have some more to eat. This beef is delicious!'

The following week Henry, Mary-Ann and Louisa made the journey back to the village. In the back of the cart Henry had his tools, several long poles and other lengths of wood.

'Do you think your Ma would like a frame either side of her door which she can lean on when she is coming in and out. I noticed her wince climbing the step.'

'Yes, the work on the farm has worn her out and she finds it difficult – and Pa as well. It's something I think the farmer should have done years ago but he won't spend any money on the cottages at all. I can remember Pa repairing the roof when I was a child. He even had to pay for the thatch and yet the farmer takes rent from them.'

'We've set off early and it's light 'til late. I should have time to do it before I leave. Then if there's anything else I'll do it when I come to pick you up.'

When they arrived at the cottage Mary-Ann's parents were not there. Knowing they would probably be returning from the nearby fields for their mid-day bread very soon, Mary-Ann directed Henry to fetch some water from the well in the village whilst she coaxed flame from the dying embers of the fire. She unpacked her bag and found the tea leaves she'd bought from Yarmouth market, knowing that her mother liked tea but could not always buy it in the village. When they arrived she was just pouring water into the tea-pot which she'd also brought: it was Mary, Robert's wife's old one which she'd given her along with some spices, as a gift for her mother.

Richard and Abigail Simms had been farm labourers all their lives. They were nearing their fortieth year and both walked with a stoop and a limp.

'What you doin' with them?' Richard asked Henry when he saw him.

'Well, I'm going to bury half of each pole in the ground then attach wood across the top with these joints,' Henry replied as he lifted some iron clasps from the cart. 'It will give you something to lean on as you get up and down your step.'

'Thar'll be good. After I've supped I'll take you to Geoff, the shearer – he'll let you wipe them poles down with a fleece or two as they come off the beasts.' Henry frowned and Richard laughed and continued. 'You've not felt a fresh fleece afore? Thick with oil them are and it'll protect them posts from the weather somewhat.'

Henry's face lit up. 'Was going to dunk them in tallow before I came but we're running low at the yard,' he replied as he loaded them back in again.

Meanwhile Mary-Ann was showing Abigail what else she had in her basket.

'Ginger!' exclaimed Abigail as soon as she saw the knobbly root. My last piece is so small that I'm sure there's no more juice in it – it has dried up. Mind I still have some left in syrup but it's nicer fresh.'

'It's a gift from Henry's aunt,' explained Mary-Ann as she took several small paper packages out of her bag, 'and there's more in here. See,' she untwisted the paper and opened it out, 'nutmeg and mace.'

Abigail laughed as she reached over for another and untwisted it. 'Cloves! Your Pa used my last on his bad tooth. He was putting off asking the vet to remove it but I met him in the village last week and asked him myself – yer Pa came in holding his mouth the following day. By then the clove had fallen apart.'

'Was Pa cross with you?'

'He grumbled a bit – but since his mouth stopped hurting he's been happier. What's inside that last one?'

Mary-Ann untwisted it but then held it closed, her eyes full of mischief. 'What would you like it to be?'

'Cinnamon?' Abigail asked hopefully and Mary-Ann opened the paper to reveal two rolls of the curled up bark. Abigail clapped her hands with glee. 'I've never had so much before. When the traders come to the village they only bring out a few thin shavings and then the price is high.'

Later, as Henry drove the cart back along the road to Yarmouth, he missed Mary-Ann and the cart was strangely silent without Louisa's chatter. As he travelled he was filled with a contentment at where his life had brought him. There was still anguish in his heart when he remembered the past but the nightmares had not recurred since he'd shared them. It was almost as if bringing them to her had removed their power. She was bearing his child and he could not imagine any of those women whose fathers had rejected him being the mother of his children. She had been hurt by her parents when they sent her away after taking her baby from her and yet she had gone to spend some time with them. A lesser person wouldn't have returned but she wanted to learn how best to care for him and his children. As he approached Yarmouth he could see the tower of St Nicholas's church and that caused him to ponder that perhaps now God had decided to start blessing him instead of sending anguish into his life. He couldn't have stopped himself smiling if he'd tried.

That evening Henry and Tom were sitting by the fireside when there was a knock on the door to their part of the house.

'Come in Rosa,' called Henry. The door opened. 'Jim! I haven't seen you for a while.'

'I've been down in Lowestoft. That's why I'm calling.' Henry noticed he was looking pale and tired. 'I've found new employment so we're leaving at the end of the week. Rosa told me you had another child coming – thought you might want to know so you can ask to take on upstairs as well. I'm sure young Tom will be pleased to come down from the attic!' Tom and Henry looked at each other and they both grinned.

'Thank you for telling us,' replied Henry, 'I think we'll take a walk round to Mr Williams now and see what he has to say. Mary-Ann will be delighted. Would you like me to ask to borrow the horse and cart again tomorrow and take you and your things down there?'

Jim's face relaxed. 'That would be wonderful,' he said, but then he frowned again. 'I have no money to pay you. We were going to walk with what we could carry and leave everything else.'

'You have no need to be in my debt, I'm pleased to help. None of us know when we will fall on hard times.'

'My Rosa will be pleased. She did not want to leave the table and the beds. Thank you so much. I'll go now and tell her.' As he left Henry and Tom stood up. They followed him out and went to see Mr Williams.

'It's nice to be coming back home again,' said Mary-Ann at the end of the following week. She glanced out across the fields they were passing and then looked back at Henry. 'Now you must tell me what it is.'

'I do not understand what you mean,' he replied. However he was unable to keep the smile from his face.

'You've been grinning since you first arrived this morning. Of course, I'm pleased that you're happy to see Louisa and me again, but I think there's something else.'

Henry laughed. 'You'll have to wait until we're home.'

Outside the main door to their house in Francis Buildings Henry took a key from his pocket. Mary-Ann looked at him in wonder: this door had never been locked before. He paused before he put it in the keyhole and looked at her. Curiosity and astonishment crossed her face.

'Have Rosa and Jim gone? Do we have the whole house?' She giggled as she realised the answer to her own question.

'Jim was taken on in Lowestoft. I borrowed the horse and cart and took them down,' he said as he opened the door. They entered the door to what had been their part of the house.

'Where are my cooking things?' Henry did not reply but instead walked through the door in the opposite wall to the room at the back which had been their sleeping room. Mary-Ann followed. She stood still at the door whilst Henry watched her delight.

'Your kitchen ma'am,' he intoned as he bowed.

'A proper cooking fire!' she exclaimed as she walked towards the small open range. Henry turned the handle to what looked like a small cupboard to one side. 'And is that an oven?' Mary-Ann clapped her hands together. 'The beds...' She followed Henry as he went upstairs and turned into a door at the top. In that room was a small bed next to which on the wall was a hook from which hung Tom's best clothes. They went through the door in the opposite wall. In that room, under the window, was their double bed and Louisa's bed was in the corner. Next to their bed was a new cradle which Henry had made. Mary-Ann went to it and pushed it gently. It rocked.

'Is this new?' she whispered as she stroked the wood.

Henry nodded. 'I made it – for our child.' Mary-Ann turned to him. He hugged her and kissed her fiercely. 'I would have some pleasure in bed with you now but it will have to wait – I must take the cart back and see to the horse.'

'And I must go to Louisa. I can hear her calling me.'

June arrived and Mary-Ann grew large. In bed Henry would rest his hands on her belly: he found it wondrous, that he had caused this and now his child was moving inside her! He felt no anxiety until, walking past a house on the way to the yard one morning, he heard a woman screaming; on his way home the screams had become weaker and intermittent. The following day he was told that she had died with her child stuck inside her. He was fearful for Mary-Ann and was glad that Abigail was coming. He wondered whether she would have known enough to help that woman and her baby. He hoped she would come soon because he did not want Mary-Ann to start to labour without her: if she did he would need to leave her for several hours to fetch Abigail. It was true that Mary, Robert's wife, had offered to stay with her if that happened but since Mary-Ann had spoken with her she said that Mary had some strange old ideas and if she was labouring hard she would not be able to stop her forcing them upon her. Henry looked for Abigail every day.

On the last Sunday in June Abigail arrived and, as she stepped down from the cart, she announced that she would stay until the baby was born unless it hadn't come by the third week of July when she would have to go back because it would be getting busy on the farm. However, when Mary-Ann stood up she looked at her shape, ran her hand over Mary-Ann's belly and told them not to worry because the babe had moved down ready to be born and it would not be long. Henry hoped she was right.

Three days later Mary-Ann started in labour. Henry left for work as usual. As he walked home at the end of the day he was anxious with anticipation. His lips were tight and his fists were clenched. When Abigail met him at the door to Francis Buildings she was smiling. Henry let out the breath he had been holding.

'A girl! I left them both sleeping.' Abigail watched Henry put his foot on the first step and hesitate. 'Go on, go up and see,' she urged. Henry bounded up the stairs. He tried to open the bedroom door quietly, but it creaked and Mary-Ann opened her eyes. Delight showed in her face as their eyes met and she looked down at the cradle; his gaze followed her.

'Pick her up.' Mary-Ann looked at Henry again. 'She's your daughter.'

'But she's asleep,' he said as he crossed the room. He crouched down next to the cradle. The baby stirred.

'Lift her out and hold her. She will want to feed soon anyway.' Carefully Henry picked up his child.

'She's so small.' The baby turned her head whilst her lips puckered. 'Look, she's moving.' The baby opened her eyes. 'Hello Caroline,' he said. He glanced at Mary-Ann who was smiling. She nodded.

'I haven't called her that yet. I wanted you to be the first to use her name.' Caroline was beginning to wriggle, her mouth opening and closing. 'I think she is hungry.' Henry watched her for a few more moments before passing her over to Mary-Ann who opened the front of her night-dress.

'Your breasts are huge!' Henry exclaimed.

'Yes, food for Caroline,' stated Mary-Ann. She held one breast and stroked the baby's face with her nipple. A drop of yellowish fluid had appeared. The baby moved her head again, found the nipple and started to feed. Tenderly Henry stroked his finger along Mary-Ann's breast and onto the baby's face. Neither parent spoke as the baby fed. Exultation expanded Henry's chest and he beamed: this was his child and he was a father.

'Are you disappointed that she is not a boy, that your first-born is not a son?' asked Mary-Ann as the baby finished feeding. Henry shook his head.

'She is my child,' he paused, looked at Mary-Ann and chuckled. 'Our child,' he corrected, 'and I am happier than I can say.' He stroked Mary-Ann's head. They looked into each other's eyes for a few moments before Mary-Ann sank back onto the pillow.

'I am tired. Take her while I sleep. I think Ma is making a broth – so hold her for a while if you want and then put her in the cradle when you are hungry.' Henry bent down and kissed Mary-Ann's forehead at the same time as lifting the baby away from the breast.

I want to protect her – to protect them both – but I've failed before. I can feel her skull, it's so fragile. An image crashed into his brain: his daughter, floppy and lifeless in his hand. What am I thinking? What's wrong with me? Shaking, he laid her in the cradle. She didn't wake. As he went downstairs he shook his head to try and rid himself of the vision.

5

Thirteen months passed.

'Look at Carrie!' Mary-Ann called out. Henry looked up to see his daughter taking her first wobbly steps.

He grinned. 'Waited to do it until she had the whole family to see.' Everyone laughed. 'She's been holding onto Mary-Ann's skirt and walking with her or pulling herself up on the legs of a chair and then letting go and standing there. We've been watching her for weeks.' Caroline stopped, looked around at her father, grinned back at him and overbalanced. Louisa quickly left her mother's side and ran to her sister. Caroline crawled away but Louisa soon caught up with her; laughing they looked at each other oblivious to all the adults in the yard who were watching them. It was mid-summer, Robert and Mary had provided a meal at the yard and all the family were there. On occasions like this, when his uncles Robert and James stood with their wives Mary and Hannah, Henry wondered what it would have been like if his parents had still been alive. They would have been the ones living in the cottage and providing a mid-summer feast for the family.

'Henry, you need to build a pen for the children,' Freddie's words cut across his thoughts. Henry frowned as he tried to work out what Freddie meant until he pointed to the scars on his face.

'There's no need,' said Mary-Ann before Henry could reply, 'Louisa knows to stay in the corner furthest from the fire and Carrie's learning quickly.'

'Do you not think I hadn't trained Frederick?' responded Hannah, Freddie's mother, her eyebrows raised towards Mary-Ann.

'I'm sure you did, Aunt,' said Henry.

'So how did it happen?' Mary-Ann asked. She paused, the two women's eyes met and everyone in the room was still. Mary-Ann continued, 'so that if we know, we might stop it happening to one of ours.'

'He was just on the edge of where I allowed them to come to,' Hannah explained, 'I was cooking. He was about the same age as Caroline and he was tired, lying on his side. The others were further in by the corner and if he'd been more awake I think I would have made him move – I've seen it many times since, in my head, and wished I had – but he was nearly asleep and I left him be.' Mary-Ann nodded. 'I'd put a fresh piece of coal on about ten minutes before and there must have been some moisture in it. Suddenly there was a loud bang and it shot off the fire and travelled a couple of yards – it was stopped by Freddie's face.'

'And if he'd been in a pen he'd have been that bit further back,' concluded Mary-Ann. She continued, turning to her husband, 'Yes, Henry, could you make a pen for them? It would be easier than having to keep watching them and the fire, especially when I'm in the back kitchen. Thank-you for telling us Aunt Hannah.' The two women smiled at each other and other conversations in the room resumed.

'Where's Rachel?' asked Tom. Henry pointed to the other side of the yard where she was talking with some of the other cousins in the family. 'I can remember when she trained us not to wander off by putting lines of driftwood that we weren't allowed to cross. A pen would be better though.'

'I'll do one next Sunday,' agreed Henry, 'are you going to help while you think it's such a good idea?'

'Of course I am – but don't you agree?'

'I do. Anything that keeps them safe. They're my children.' Henry's voice suddenly had a hardness and some people looked round at him but he did not notice as he went off to find some ale.

Four months passed. Mary-Ann was sitting by the fire replacing the cuffs on one of Henry's shirts.

'I'll be back soon. I just want to go and see something,' said Henry as he poked his head in through the door. It was Saturday afternoon and, as it wasn't his turn to supervise the apprentices whilst they cleared away the debris of the week's work at the yard, he was home early.

'Sit down and have some bread first,' suggested Mary-Ann. Henry looked back over his shoulder. He was undecided.

'Pa, Pa!' Louisa called. Caroline looked up at her sister's call and her eyes opened wide at the sight of her father. She smiled. It was enough to stop Henry and, in two steps, he was by the pen. Both girls held their arms up to him.

'Now how do I choose which one of you to pick up first?' Henry crouched down, reached into the pen and lifted out Louisa.

'Now hold onto me,' he said as he balanced her on his knee and reached into the pen for Caroline. He stood up with both of them and sat down on the bench by the table.

'So where were you going?' Mary-Ann asked as she put some bread and a cup of tea on the table in front of him.

'To the railway,' he replied and Mary-Ann nodded.

'I should have guessed.'

'I heard today that they've started running trains between Yarmouth and Reedham – they're carrying ballast for the rest of the train track.' Both of the girls now had a piece of bread each and he kissed their foreheads before putting them back in the pen. 'I can't wait to see a moving steam engine,' he added as he drained the last of his tea and moved towards the door.

'Fish for your dinner tonight,' said Mary-Ann and he looked back and grinned.

Fifteen minutes later he was crossing the bridge over the river Bure. He looked up at the chains by which it was suspended over the water, remembering when it was built. Hall's had won the contract but they'd needed help and had come to Spandler's. Hall's had had a photograph taken of them all on the bridge and he recalled how long they'd had to stand still.

'Good-day Mr Cray,' he said as he paid his halfpenny toll. He stepped off the bridge and, for a few moments, stood and watched. On the water was a boat upon which men shovelled ballast into a huge bucket attached to a crane. He watched as the crane lifted its load into the air and turned to lower it into an open carriage, one of several attached to an engine further up the single track which had been laid out across the marshes where, years earlier, he had skated with William. He frowned as he tried to work out what was powering the crane because there were no men pulling on ropes. Then, on the carriage, other men emptied the bucket. Next to the track men were in trenches digging out foundations for a building. Henry walked along beside the track and stopped next to the engine: it was hissing gently. He watched while men loaded on more coal and added water to the tank. With Henry's knowledge of steam engines he soon worked out how the engine moved along the track and as he watched them building up the fire he realised that they were preparing the engine to move. He looked to the end of the train: the men were emptying the bucket into the last carriage. He started to smile as the hissing increased. Five minutes passed and thick smoke spurted from the funnel. Under the train he could see flames from the fire and the smoke from the funnel became lighter as it was replaced by steam. The train began to move. The exhaust from the funnel turned back to smoke and as it did the chug chug sound it produced matched the pounding of Henry's heart. It moved off over the marshes and whistled whilst Henry stared until it disappeared, and quietness returned.

'Amazing sight, is it not?' The voice made Henry jump.

'Good-day to you again Mr Cray. Certainly it is! I hadn't realised you had followed me from the bridge.'

'Have you seen the crane?'

'Yes, how does it lift?'

'Something to do with water,' he shrugged. 'They did show me but I did not understand. I expect you would though. Come and see, they're so proud of their new crane that they'll want to show you.' As they walked towards the crane the men waved.

'Last train of the day?' Mr Cray asked. The men grinned as they straightened up and leant on their shovels.

'That's the last bucket. We'll just move it onto the quayside so the ship can go back to be loaded up ready for tomorrow.' Looking around the crane Henry spotted a small steam engine but he could see that it wasn't big enough to lift the bucket, which was huge. He estimated there to be forty cubic feet of stone in there! Then one man turned a wheel on one side of the crane.

'Closed!' he called and another man turned a different wheel on the other side of the crane. Henry held his breath as the bucket rose into the air. The men jumped off the boat and swung the crane so that the bucket was suspended above the ground. The men turned the wheels again and the bucket descended.

'This is Henry, one of the Spandler millwrights,' Mr Cray was introducing him to one of the men. Henry's eyes moved between the man and the crane. The man grinned.

'You're trying to work out how it works?' he asked. Henry nodded. 'Well, we've finished for the day now so we'll empty it.' He nodded to one of the men who turned just one of the wheels. Water bubbled up in the river under the crane and, for the first time, Henry saw a pipe running from the crane to the river which was also attached to the steam engine. His frown dissipated and his eyes lit up.

'It's the water powering the crane!' he exclaimed. 'You must pump water to the top of the crane until it's heavier than the stones and then,' he paused and his frown returned for a moment before he continued, 'then when you want to lower it you must let some water out so that the stones are heavier.'

A few minutes later Mr Cray and Henry we're walking back to the bridge together.

'You are clever people you Spandlers. I couldn't work out what he was saying when he explained it to me and yet you worked it out for yourself.' He paused. 'I wonder if you could work something out for me. I need the bridge to be bigger.' Henry frowned.

'What, take it down and build another?'

'No, just make it a bit wider – add a footpath to each side so that there's room on the main bridge for two carts to pass.' Henry stood still and looked at the bridge for a few minutes.

'I-I'm not sure,' he stuttered. 'I know suspension bridges are very finely balanced with the weight on the chains and the anchors in the banks.' He looked up at the chains as he spoke and then carried on walking. 'I'll ask the other millwrights. I suppose you're expecting a great deal more traffic when the railway opens?' Mr Cray nodded.

'It's my good fortune that the railway has chosen to come to this part of Yarmouth.' He was speaking faster and Henry sensed his excitement. He reminded him of Louisa when he came back from work with a sweet pastry from Boulter's and she wanted it. 'My grandfather had the ferry crossing here and my father was given permission to build the bridge. They didn't know that the railways would come, but they're coming and I shall make a good deal of money from the extra tolls.' Mr Cray rubbed his hands together in glee. 'However, I need the extra width on the bridge.' He turned to face Henry and his eyes narrowed.

'I don't know if it's possible.' Henry spoke quietly but with precise articulation.

Mr Cray folded his arms and pouted his lip in the same way that Louisa did when Henry said no. Henry suppressed a laugh.

'It's my right.' Mr Cray's voice was hard. Henry, realising that he wanted an argument, ignored the challenge.

'I shall ask at the yard but for now I must be returning home. Good-day to you.' Henry turned and walked back over the bridge, pausing in the middle and looking down at the swirling water. It looked dark; suddenly he felt cold and his breath stopped in his chest. People did not like to be on the bridge when it was busy because it wobbled sometimes, and he remembered, when it was first opened, standing in the market place next to his father whilst his grandfather tried to convince some of the townsfolk of its safety. He exhaled and shivered, shrugging his shoulders to dispel his uneasiness. Then he laughed at his own disquiet knowing that his grandfather would say he should go away and think through the problem rather than reacting like a superstitious washerwoman. As he walked back he wondered what Robert would make of Mr Cray's idea and tried to think about it logically. However, when he reached to open his front door he noticed that his hand still shook. His sense of foreboding had not disappeared.

As Henry walked into the yard the following Monday, Robert was standing by the door to the cottage.

'Time to talk?' Henry asked. Robert nodded and turned back into the cottage.

'What is it that is troubling my favourite nephew?'

'Not so much troubling,' replied Henry, disregarding the memories of his feeling on the bridge. 'It's just something you need to know about.'

'Sit down.' Robert pointed to the leather chair by the fire before sitting down behind his desk.

'I went for a walk, to see one of the new trains.'

'Yes, I've been to see them. Life is going to change, you know.'

Henry nodded. 'It's all very exciting, but that's not what I came to talk about. Whilst I was there Mr Cray spoke with me. Said he wanted to make the bridge wider. Can it be done?'

Robert shook his head as he thought, and then said, 'It's very tall and narrow, that's why it wobbles so easily. But how does he think it will happen? Take it down and build a new one?'

It was Henry's turn to shake his head. 'No, he just wants to add a footpath each side of it.'

'I think you could probably build a wider one at that point but that one is old. Wonder what Hall's would think?'

Three days later and work had ceased for the day. Robert and James, with the other millwrights and apprentices, were sitting at the workbenches waiting the arrival of the ironworkers from Hall's.

'What's this about?' Edmund demanded. 'It's the end of the day. I want to go indoors.'

'Can't wait to go to your Ma? And your dinner?' asked Freddie. Edmund scowled at him whilst others smiled.

'You'll find out soon enough,' said Robert. 'Henry here has something to tell us that is important to our business and Hall's'.

'Henry!' snorted Edmund, heaving himself up from the stool he was sitting on. He turned to his father, wide-eyed, sweat running down his jowls. 'I'm your son. Why have you not told me? I should make the announcement rather than him!' Edmund pointed angrily at Henry. A group of five men entered the yard and everyone turned from Edmund to look in their direction.

'Thanks for coming,' said Robert, shaking the hand of the oldest man in the group. Mr Hall nodded.

'Why have your called us over?'

'Henry,' said Robert as he turned to his nephew. Henry explained Mr Cray's request to everyone.

'That's good,' said Edmund when Henry stopped speaking and looked round. 'More business, more money for us both. Don't you agree Mr Hall?'

'Edmund!' Robert's voice was sharp. 'I'll remind you that you're a junior millwright here. Your opinion was not asked for.' Robert turned to Mr Hall, 'I apologise for my son. What do you think?'

'I'd be happier if we could at least replace the chains, although that's a big job in itself. Do you know Mr Cray has been in touch with the original architect?' Everyone looked surprised. 'He's been to see me as well – when I received your message I thought that this was what it would be about. Apparently the architect has told him that the bridge had been designed to take more weight than originally expected so the addition of a pathway should not affect it.'

'I'm surprised at that,' said Robert. 'Does the architect know he plans to put the footpaths on the edge of the bridge, outside the square drop of the chains?'

'That I cannot answer, not having spoken to him myself,' Mr Hall continued, 'however, perhaps he thought that a footpath would be very narrow and so not have much of an effect. That said I'd feel happier if the chains were renewed, or at least re-tested.'

Robert nodded. 'I agree but I do not think Mr Cray will – that would be costly and put the bridge out of action whilst the chains were down.' Henry, remembering the way Mr Cray rubbed his hands together at the thought of how much money he would make, nodded.

'I'm sure he won't,' said Henry, 'because he can only see the increased income the wider bridge would give him. If the architect has told him it will work, he'll not be interested in extra expense – and renewing the chains would add much to our charge to him.'

James, Robert's brother, spoke. 'I think that, if we are to do the work, we need to make it clear to him that we would want to replace the chains – and also we need his assurance that the architect has agreed to all the changes.'

'And if he says no,' Henry shrugged, 'I would say we should not do the work. I would like to talk with the architect directly ourselves before we agree.'

'I was hoping for a decision today,' said Mr Hall. 'We have discussed it at our yard and although, like I said, I would be happier if the chains were tested, we have decided we want to do it.'

Robert looked from his brother, James, to Henry: uncertainty showed on both their faces.

'I expected that we would agree to do this,' stated Robert, 'but others are more cautious and have made me reconsider. I will come to you with our decision before the end of the week.' Mr Hall nodded and he and his men left the yard.

'Pa!' Edmund exploded, 'are you the millwright in charge or not? Why do you not stick to your own decisions? Clearly you thought that the work was something we should do when you invited Hall's over but you have allowed yourself to be dissuaded by my cousin. Why do you tell me to be quiet and yet allow Henry to speak? He is no more a senior millwright than I am.' He turned to Henry. 'I say that you should justify to us all here and now your reasons for persuading my father to hesitate. You only work here but I will inherit this business one day and I want it to be profitable. You,' Edmund jabbed his finger at Henry, 'do not care!'

'Edmund!' Robert exclaimed.

'It's okay,' said Henry calmly, 'I do care – but he's right, I should give my reasons. As it stands now the bridge is unstable.' Everyone nodded: the vibrations that happened when the bridge was busy were well known. 'My understanding of suspension bridges is that the weight must be inside the chains. It is, at the moment, and yet it still wobbles. I cannot see that the addition of footpaths will improve it – in fact I suspect that they will make it unusable.'

'But the architect has said that he agrees with the addition of a pathway!' Edmund shouted, his podgy face red, the perspiration making lines through the grime of his day's work.

'So Mr Hall told us,' Henry replied, 'and he said he knew that because Mr Cray had told him. However, Mr Cray doesn't think about anything other than profit. Like I said before, we should see what the architect says, speak to him directly, before we agree to this.'

'Edmund,' interjected Robert, 'you may be my son but your comments when Henry first explained what Mr Cray had asked show that you are only interested in the money that can be made.' He gave a short laugh before continuing, 'and thus you are of like mind with Mr Cray. However, you need to look on a job with the eyes of a millwright – which Henry does. He is experienced and knowledgeable and,' he turned to Henry, 'yes, strictly speaking your uncle and I are the senior millwrights, but I have to say that I often forget that you're my nephew and not my brother.' Henry's face lit up and Robert, James and Henry grinned at each other. The other men there, including Freddie and Jim who had been Henry's apprentices and Tom, Henry's brother, smiled. Edmund scowled and stomped off, backside wobbling, into the cottage.

'Come and have some ale with us,' Robert suggested as he, James, Henry, and Tom left the yard together. Henry hesitated.

'I'll tell Mary-Ann,' said Tom. 'Go and spend some time with the old men now that Uncle Robert has included you!' Tom's eyes danced.

'Impudence!' retorted Henry as he followed Robert and James into the King's Arms and Tom left them, chuckling as he went.

Part way through his second tankard Henry began to have doubts.

'What if Edmund is right? He voiced the question. Robert shrugged.

'Like you, my instinct is that it would make the bridge even more unstable than it is now. However, I would also admit that we do not understand completely the forces at work and time may prove me – us both – wrong.'

6

'Mary-Ann, will you marry me?' Henry's eyes were bright. Mary-Ann was leaning over the pen where she had been wiping the girls' faces. She looked up with a frown.

'Of course. What do you mean? We decided that many years ago.'

'I mean will you marry me now – or rather in the new year when I've made the arrangements. We have two children and we can afford it now.' Mary-Ann's frown transformed into a beam.

'I will be Mrs Spandler!' Henry crossed the room, put his arm round her waist and drew her close to him. She felt slender beneath his arm and he was aware of his strength. His wife: he felt as if his smile was wide enough to split his face in two.

The next day Henry went to see Robert.

'I have the money for the church fees and I would like to marry Mary-Ann after Christmas.'

'I'm pleased. It will be good, when you have your first son, for him to be born a Spandler according to law.' He turned to the shelves behind his desk, lifted off an old wooden box and blew. A cloud of dust was propelled towards the window. 'This hasn't been opened since your Uncle James married your Aunt Hannah!' Henry was smiling.

'Thank-you Uncle Robert. I had wondered…' His voice trailed off.

'You're a Spandler, no matter what your father did. Spandlers always marry with one of our special rings.' He opened the box and drew out a mould which he handed to Henry. He reached into the box again and lifted out two small parcels, each wrapped in a greasy cloth.

'Are those the metals?' Robert nodded.

'Yes, copper and zinc. Don't need much of the zinc, just enough to make it harder so that it will last. You don't want it changing shape the first time she lifts the kettle from the fire!' They both laughed. Henry unclipped the two halves of the mould and pulled them apart. Inside were six small ring-shaped holes, each in its own shallow depression. Robert handed him a cloth bag. Henry opened it and rolled six dull, grey rings out into his palm. He looked at Robert.

'Your grandfather made them when he first made the mould. Take them home and let Mary-Ann try them then tie some thread around the one that fits her best. The outsides are very rough but the insides have been smoothed so they'll not hurt her.' Henry nodded and tipped them back into the bag again.

'Thank-you again,' said Henry.

'It's good to see you so happy. Mary-Ann is a good, strong woman. I'll admit I was unsure at first.'

'Because of her family?'

'Yes, she is lower than we usually wed. But then...' Henry's smile faded and Robert quickly continued, 'that does not matter. She has a quickness about her which I like and you two will do well together.'

'I did try to find others. I thought that if I could marry someone with some money then perhaps I could buy my way back in here.' The two men looked at each other, then Henry smiled. 'I don't think your Edmund would be very happy at that.' They both laughed.

It was early in the morning of the second Sunday in January, the day that Henry had arranged to marry Mary-Ann.

'Hello, I've come for the girls,' said Rachel as Tom let her in.

'Thank-you for coming,' said Mary-Ann as she looked through from the kitchen. Rachel laughed.

'Well, if I hadn't Tom would be looking after them.' Rachel looked at her younger brother who grinned back at her.

'Yes, they're far better off with you here. I don't have any idea about getting little girls dressed.'

'I'll bring them to the yard, later, when you all get back from church,' said Rachel and Mary-Ann nodded. 'To think, the next time I see you, you will be a Spandler!' Tom and Rachel stood either side of Mary-Ann and each of them put an arm around her.

'I'm so glad that you are becoming Henry's wife – and so becoming our sister,' said Tom. 'It's nice to have a new member of our family.' At that moment Henry came through the door that led to the stairs.

'Did I hear someone mention a new member of our family?' He raised his eyebrows at Mary-Ann. She laughed.

'Yes, but not what you think. I haven't told them that.'

'We were talking about Mary-Ann becoming one of us,' explained Rachel. She looked from Mary-Ann to Henry and back whilst they looked at each other and Mary-Ann giggled.

'Mary-Ann has just realised that she is with child again,' said Henry. I thought today couldn't be better – until she told me. But we'd best be going. We don't want to keep the vicar waiting.'

'I've never been to church this early on a Sunday!' exclaimed Mary-Ann as they walked towards the town. 'It's cold – look at the ice in those puddles.'

'It is January!' exclaimed Henry. 'I'm pleased it's cold because the drain does not smell as bad.' They had reached the place where planks had been laid across the ditch to form a bridge. 'It almost seems as if it was someone else who lived down there,' he said looking down Garrison Walk. Mary-Ann squeezed his arm.

'That's good. Don't try and remember it. This is your life now and we're being wed today.' Henry gave a small skip and they both laughed. They walked on past the place where North Gate had stood, past the door to the Spandler's millwrights' yard and along by the railings around St Nicholas's churchyard. They were just making their way between the trees on church plain when Mary-Ann suddenly stopped, pulling back on Henry so he couldn't go forward.

'What's wrong?' There was panic in his eyes which Mary-Ann saw.

'Don't worry, I still want to wed you. It's just that there is a spider's web between those two trees. It'll be an old one from last year but look, it's beautiful where the frost has touched it.'

'Yes, but it's time Mary-Ann.' He went to move forward but she held onto him.

'We must go around the tree. We can't break the spider's web. Not today, of all days.' Henry looked perplexed. 'My Ma would tell you,' explained Mary-Ann, 'that it will spoil our time to come if we break it.'

'Perhaps that's what my Pa did on his way to London,' said Henry as they went through the gates into the churchyard.

'Yes, but you didn't – it didn't happen to you,' whispered Mary-Ann as they entered through the South Door of the church.

'The vicar said to wait by the altar,' said Henry as he strode down the aisle. Mary-Ann clung onto his arm as they approached. Although she had now been in this church many times it still filled her with awe. 'I wonder where he is?'

'It's strange, this church,' whispered Mary-Ann, 'why did they build walls in it? It would be wonderful if it was opened up.'

'Perhaps, but it's been like that for as long as anyone can remember. They did it centuries ago when the Puritans and the Presbyterians wanted to worship as well.'

'Yes, but no-one uses those parts now.' She stopped because Henry had nudged her. The black-cloaked vicar approached.

Two strangers stood beside Henry and Mary-Ann as they said their vows and afterwards, while the vicar went off to prepare for the morning service, they led them into the vestry to sign the register. Henry was shocked to discover that his wife could not even write her name and signed with a cross.

During the service that followed Mary-Ann kept fiddling with the ring on her finger. It felt strange, as if her finger was bigger than usual. She was happy that, although she'd sat in the Spandler pew before, this time her name was Spandler and it was where she was supposed to be.

At the yard Robert's wife, Mary, and her serving girl had produced platters of cold meats and fish, bread and cheese and great bowls of salad. In the centre was the bride pie.

'Look at that!' exclaimed Henry as he and Mary-Ann approached the table. Mary-Ann smiled.

'It's beautiful.' She traced her fingers over the hard, shiny, dark-brown crust into which had been inlaid a figure of a man and a woman.

'Look,' pointed Henry, 'that must be me – I'm holding some tools – and you seem to have a bunch of plants. It must be twenty-four inches across!' They looked up and Mary, Robert's wife, was standing by the table watching them.

'Yes, far too big for my oven,' she said. 'Boulter's baked it for me and even loaned me the tin as none of mine were large enough. They offered to make it for me but I wanted to do it as a welcome for you.' She looked into Mary-Ann's eyes and they both smiled.

'Th-th-thank-you,' Mary-Ann stuttered. Mary moved round the table to Mary-Ann's side, put her arm around her, and hugged her.

'Welcome to the family Mrs Spandler,' she laughed, 'I remember when I first became a Spandler.' They looked at each other and Mary-Ann smiled.

'Thank-you,' Henry said to Robert as the family helped themselves to the food, 'Mary-Ann and I appreciate your generosity.'

'It's my pleasure,' his uncle replied, 'and it's a small thing for my favourite nephew. It gives me great delight to see you so happy, although it's not just us you need to thank – Mr Greensome at the nursery provided the salad.' Although eight years had passed since Hannah's death following an accident at the nursery, sudden grief caused Henrys breath to judder. Robert put a hand on Henry's shoulder. 'His intention was to add to the feast, not to cause you distress.' Henry shook himself and looked at his uncle.

'I know. It just overwhelms me sometimes. It's worse when I don't expect it.' He forced a small smile and Mary-Ann squeezed his arm. He turned to her and his smile widened. 'It's just as well that now I have you.' Robert laughed and put his other arm on Mary-Ann's shoulder.

'You will do well, both of you – and your own children will give you joy to lessen your grief.' They turned to look at Louisa and Caroline who were playing with two stick figures that Freddie and James had just given them.

'They certainly do that,' agreed Henry, 'and Mary-Ann told me last night that another child has started inside her.'

'That's wonderful news,' said Robert, 'perhaps this time the baby will be a brother for the girls?'

'Who knows,' laughed Mary-Ann, 'only when time goes by, and I have my birthing, will we have the answer that question. Please excuse me,' she said as she removed her hand from Henry's arm, 'I must go and help Rachel.' She was looking over the shoulders of the two men who immediately turned around to see. Mary-Ann laughed: Caroline and Louisa were holding Rachel's hands and pulling her towards the tables of food.

'I think the girls are hungry,' Henry said.

As she walked away Robert and Henry were joined by Robert's brother, James, together with James's sons, Jim and Freddie.

'Have you heard?' James asked. 'The railway company have failed in their bid to build a new bridge across the Bure. Blocked by Mr Cray, of course.'

'Odd, that bridge of his. Since the footpaths were added either side it does not seem to wobble as much,' commented Henry.

Robert nodded. 'It's almost as if he's improved it by accident, which shows that we don't really understand how suspension bridges work. I honestly expected the footpath to make it worse.'

'Well then, it's a pity we changed our minds and didn't work with Hall's on the contract, isn't it?' Everyone turned around. Edmund had joined them and he continued, 'all the money goes to them now and we could have had a share in it.' His podgy lips were pursed and his cheeks were red. Henry thought it made him look as if he was a large, squashed tomato and he had to suppress a laugh.

'As I've just said,' Robert looked sharply at his son, 'we do not understand everything about the forces involved. The work appears to have stabilised it but I still think that we made the right decision. As it is now it is unbalanced.'

Edmund raised his eyes to the sky. 'You sound just like Henry. Why do you listen to him? Why not listen to me sometimes – I am your son and this time I was right. We shouldn't have backed out of doing the work. It would have been money in the yard. We could have expanded, made the business bigger.'

'So that when you bury your father your share will fetch a higher price? You know that that would be the best thing for you to do – sell up – because your understanding is flawed,' said Jim. His brother Freddie nodded but frowned as well, causing the scars where his eye would have been to move to the top of his head. No-one watching him could stop themselves from smiling. Freddie laughed. 'Why can I never be serious?' Everyone was laughing with him – except Edmund who was perspiring heavily. He breathed in deeply and pulled himself up to his full height: unfortunately it still left him half a head shorter than everyone else.

'The yard did not take part in the bridge improvements because you all felt it wouldn't work. My opinion was not listened to,' he turned towards Robert, 'and I am your son. Your son,' he repeated, his voice louder this time, 'and will be in your position one day.' He glared at them all.

'God help us,' muttered Freddie. Edmund turned on him jabbing a finger in his direction.

'You say my abilities are flawed,' then he pointed to himself, 'but I-I wanted us to be part of that contract. And I was right – we'd have made money from it.'

'Yes, it appears that you were right,' his father Robert admitted, 'and I can see that you know when there is money to be made,' Edmund nodded and smiled, looking round at everyone for their approval – but his smile froze as his father continued, 'it was a risk that Hall's took and they were lucky because nobody knew whether it would work.' Edmund's smile faded and the colour drained from his face. 'They could just as easily have lost a great deal and I know one thing – if it had made the bridge unusable Mr Cray would not have paid for the work and may even have sued them for damaging his bridge.' Robert looked at his son. Edmund stared back at him then let his eyes move over the group who were watching, some of whom were already smirking. He let out the breath he'd been holding with an explosive whoosh and huffed across the yard and into the cottage.

For a few moments there was silence.

'Perhaps he'll change as he matures more,' suggested James.

'I've been saying something similar myself since he was five or six.' Robert shrugged. 'If he applied himself, then maybe he would learn, but I am not hopeful.' He turned to Henry. 'Would that your Pa were alive – or at least that he'd not sold his share.' Henry gave a short laugh which stuck in his throat. 'The yard, this business that our Pa built up from nothing,' Robert continued, glancing at James, his brother, 'it would have come to you, Henry, to a safe pair of hands. What will become of Spandler's after I've gone I just don't know.'

James clapped him on the back. 'That won't be for some time yet.'

'I wonder what our women are talking about,' observed Henry looking at the door of the cottage to where Mary-Ann was standing with Hannah, wife of James. Mary, Robert's wife, had just followed Edmund indoors. Rachel was with them, holding the hands of Louisa and Carrie. Louisa was smiling at Hannah. Carrie saw her father and he beckoned to her. She pulled on Rachel's arm and Rachel looked up and let her go. She toddled unsteadily to Henry who picked her up. She reached towards him and pulled on his hair where it was falling forward.

'Be careful Henry,' called James, 'that's how I lost mine, when the children pulled on it!' Henry laughed but still reached round with his free hand and untangled Carrie's fingers. Father and daughter looked into each other's eyes and Henry felt a pressure of happiness like the steam in Bessie except that he did not want to find the valve to release the pressure. He didn't mind if he exploded with joy.

'We were watching Richard and George playing with our girls,' Mary-Ann explained when they moved over to join them. 'That's until Edmund stormed past. Aunt Mary was cross. Did you upset him?'

'Our George and your Richard are growing tall, Robert,' observed Hannah, 'and they seem to be the best of friends.' At that moment Mary came back out of the cottage.

'It's a pity you two,' she looked directly at Freddie and Jim, 'cannot befriend Edmund. After all you are cousins.'

'As am I, Aunt Mary,' said Henry, 'but he is difficult to get along with. Very different to Freddie and Jim – and Richard and George.'

'Your Richard's a great lad,' said Freddie, 'I am looking forward to working with him at the yard in a few years. But Ed? Well he's different, hard to work alongside.'

'I don't know what you all have against him,' Mary said, glaring at her husband. 'Yes, you as well. Edmund's right you know, you do favour Henry here above your own son.' She turned and went back indoors.

'Henry, Mary-Ann,' Thomas spoke softly between them, 'I have something for you. Come over here.' He led them over to one of the workbenches, reached behind it and drew out a rectangular package wrapped in brown paper.

'It's a frame!' Mary-Ann exclaimed as Henry removed the paper. Henry smiled at his wife as he took the wedding certificate from his jacket pocket.

'The corners of the frame are beautifully mitred,' Henry grinned at younger brother, 'and it should fit well. Thank-you.'

'When I told Uncle Robert what I was going to do he said I could help myself to whatever offcuts I could find. I did it after work when you'd gone home.'

'I wondered why you were so late back the last few nights,' said Mary-Ann.

'Are we going to eat this pie then?' called Freddie from over by the food. They walked back and Henry helped Mary-Ann cut open the pie: inside it was filled with apples and quinces. As the serving girl distributed the pieces Henry noticed that Edmund had reappeared.

'Are you enjoying the pie, Ed?' he asked. Edmund nodded. There was so much pie in his mouth that his lips would not close and he was frantically trying to swallow. Henry added, 'it's good to know that you wish us well.' At this Edmund spluttered and Jim and Freddie, who were standing behind him, grinned.

Back at Francis Buildings Henry hung the frame above their bed. That night they stood either side of the bed and looked at each other. Henry looked at the certificate, leaned across the bed and grasped Mary-Ann's hand.

'Come with me, Mrs Spandler,' he said and they laughed as they fell towards each other into the bed.

7

'As you may know, the railway is to have its official opening on the thirtieth of April. Spandler's yard will open for work on that day and I expect you to be here as usual.' There was a groan from all the men, followed by muttering. Robert raised his arm and they were quiet. He smiled. 'On that day it is only the really important people who can use the train. On the day after, however, anyone can buy a ticket – and I have.' He paused, and the men looked at each other. 'I have bought tickets for all of us.' The collective gasp was like a release of steam. He continued, 'Spandler's yard will be closed for the morning – we will be on the train that leaves Yarmouth at eight and we should be back here not long after mid-day. That is why, on the day of the opening, we will work as usual.'

That day dawned fair and the first journey by train between Norwich and Yarmouth did not pass un-noticed: the civic dignitaries, who travelled first class, were served refreshments in the station-master's rooms and then were taken by horse-drawn omnibus through the town to the beach and jetty, but those of lesser rank, who only had second and third-class tickets, had to find their own sustenance and entertainment in the town. It was the first opportunity for the people of Yarmouth to make money out of the coming of the railway: fish sellers lit fires and cooked herring, the smell of which enticed the customers; the public houses opened wide their doors; entertainers tossed skittles in the air and walked on stilts and, amongst them all, surreptitiously, the dishonest of Yarmouth relieved the visitors of objects of value. At the yard, as the men worked, the talk was of nothing else but the railway.

'My grandmother has told me not to go,' said one of the apprentices, 'she says that it's too fast – that our bowels will fall out!' Everyone laughed.

'I have heard other old ones in the town say that – or else that the train will not be able to stop and will fall into the river,' said Freddie.

'It's not just the old ones. A young man asked me last night how strong the driver was,' said James.

'Yes, I was there,' laughed his son, Jim, 'and would you believe that he thought the engine would have reins like a horse and the driver would have to shout "Woah!" to stop the train!'

'I do wonder if it will make us dizzy or ill,' suggested Edmund. Some of the men smirked.

'But you've heard of other places where they already have the railways, Edmund? If things like that were happening they wouldn't be building any more,' explained James as he glanced at Robert. There were a few titters. Edmund coloured as sweat oozed onto his forehead. He puffed out his next breath.

'Anyway, where's Henry this morning?' he blustered, looking around, 'I thought my father said we all had to be at work. Has he sneaked off to look at the railway?'

'No, actually,' retorted Thomas, 'your father's sent him down to the quay to look over our next delivery of tree trunks. They've arrived at last but there's some question about the quality.'

Edmund turned. 'He could send me sometimes,' he muttered as he went into the cottage.

'Uncle Robert's going to receive a complaint I think,' suggested Thomas.

'Yes – and he will have cause to make a complaint if he comes out here and finds you all still standing round Bessie,' said James. 'It'll be half way through the morning shortly!' Everyone grinned and turned to their workbenches.

Later that evening Henry was in the King's Arms. Jim and Freddie arrived and joined him, followed moments later by James and Robert who went and sat in one of the booths.

After few minutes Edmund arrived, short of breath and perspiring as usual. For a few moments he stood looking bewildered. He caught sight of his father and James in the booth but still looked around the room. Finally, he saw Henry, Jim and Freddie.

'Thought I'd better join you, so I can hear what subject you're going to talk about tomorrow. Then I can try and think of things to say that won't make people laugh at me.'

'You're welcome to join us, Ed,' said Jim, 'but why do you make it sound as if we're plotting against you?'

'It feels like that. This morning you talked about the railway because you knew I didn't know much about it.' Henry, Jim and Freddie looked at each other and raised their eyebrows. No-one spoke. Henry took a drink from his tankard and a moment later Jim and Freddie drank from theirs. Edmund gave a short laugh. 'You even copy him when he drinks.'

'Like Jim said, you're welcome to join us – but be pleasant,' advised Freddie.

'Oh, it's all very pleasant with you isn't it?' Edmund's tone was mocking as he continued: 'Remember this – one day I will be the millwright in charge of Spandler's yard. Then no-one will be laughing at me, least of all my cousins. Of that I am sure.' His eyes moved from one to the other as he spoke. Freddie frowned and the scars on his face moved, causing Henry and Jim to smile. 'You needn't smile at me,' Edmund continued, 'I'm serious. You need to change the way you treat me.'

'Ed,' said Henry, 'we were smiling at Freddie. He looks funny when he frowns and it makes us smile. It's true, you say things and it makes the men at the yard laugh. But we don't plot how to make you do it. It's just that sometimes you say things that are foolish.'

'Whatever made you think that the railway would make us ill?' Freddie asked. 'It's the sort of comment my mother would say.' Edmund folded his arms, pushed his lips together and looked at the floor.

'I'm looking forward to the trip tomorrow,' said Henry. 'We're meeting at the railway. Did Robert say at half past seven?' he asked.

'Yes,' said Jim.

'You won't always belittle me,' Edmund muttered. 'I will have my revenge.' He looked up and shouted, 'I will be in charge and you will have to respect what I say.' He stood and stomped across the room to the door. Henry went to go after him as Robert and James looked out of the booth. Robert met Henry's eyes; he shrugged and went back to his ale and Henry sat down.

'Another grand exit,' said Freddie, 'perhaps he should be on the stage?'

'Let him go, I say.' Jim picked up his tankard. 'Here's to tomorrow and our trip on the railway.' Henry grinned and finished the last of his tankard.

'I must go – Mary-Ann will have my dinner ready. Just as well Robert's had us work twice as hard today. I'm so excited that if I wasn't so tired I probably wouldn't sleep!'

'Mary-Ann's a good wife – I'm sure she'll help you sleep,' said Jim. He and Freddie winked at each other and laughed.

'Here comes Mr Spandler with the tickets,' called out one of the men the following morning as Robert came into sight. He was followed by Edmund.

'Almost looks as if he's had to drag Ed along,' Thomas said. Freddie and Jim glanced at him and nodded. Henry didn't look: he had decided that he was going to ignore Edmund today. He was only going to think about trains and was impatient to be on the platform and watch the engine being brought up to steam. Then they would climb into a carriage and travel faster than any of them had ever travelled before. Henry jumped from one foot to the other making Thomas, Jim and Freddie laugh just as Edmund joined them.

'Now we remember what you were like as a boy, Henry!' Jim clapped him on the back and Henry stopped jumping up and down and grinned. Edmund looked confused and Freddie saw him.

'Did you think we were laughing at you?' he asked. 'No, we were laughing at Henry and he's laughing with us. Taking it with good humour as you need to learn to do.'

'Look, Uncle Robert is calling us over to him,' said Jim. They went to Robert who gave them all a ticket. As they walked into the station to the train Henry was skipping. Whilst Robert and the other men boarded the train, Henry went to look at the engine and he was followed by Thomas, Freddie and Jim. Henry explained what he knew about the parts, comparing it with the yard's small, stationary steam engine.

'Time to board gentlemen,' a guard said. Henry, Thomas, Jim and Freddie walked along the platform.

'There they are, in that open carriage,' said Henry.

'Pa's saved us seats,' said Freddie as they climbed in. They sat in the space on the wooden bench as the guard closed and locked the doors.

'Can you believe my Pa's making us travel third class?' Edmund snorted in disgust. He was not sitting along the edge of the carriage with all the other men but on the bench that ran down the centre.

'Your Pa's been very kind to buy us tickets,' Henry's face was unsmiling, 'so stop complaining or get off now and go home to your Ma.'

'My Pa won't let me. I didn't want to come but he insisted.'

'Well I want to enjoy this trip without listening to you whining – so only speak if you've got something to say that's worth listening to.' All the other men who heard Henry nodded and someone called out 'Hear, hear!'

'Look,' someone else called out, 'there's more smoke coming out of the funnel – and now it's turning white!'

'It's the steam,' shouted Henry, 'we're about to move.' Slowly, the engine pulled the train along the platform. Everyone grinned. As the train picked up speed Henry took off his cap: bits of soot were falling from the engine and he used it to shield his face. Others copied him.

'Something's in my eye,' wailed Edmund but no-one took any notice of him.

'There's Collingsworth's pump,' shouted Freddie, 'it took us a long time to walk there last week but we only left the station five minutes ago!' Henry's eyes were wide. He'd never moved across the marshes so quickly before. He looked over towards Yarmouth and was astonished how small it appeared. After about twenty minutes they approached a large village.

'It looks as if they're building on the river.'

'It must be Reedham.'

'Already!'

'Yes. I heard they're going to put a line in to Lowestoft. Apparently it's a swing bridge so the boats can get through,' explained Robert. 'The railways won't be stopped!' The train drew into Reedham station. The men watched as crates were unloaded from the last carriage of the train.

'Be fish I expect,' said James, 'and I'll wager they've never had it so fresh!' The guard came past the carriage checking the doors were locked although no-one had left or entered since Yarmouth.

'Anyone for Reedham?' he asked, looking over the sides of the open carriage. 'Next stop is Cantley.'

'Cantley!' echoed Mr Gough, one of the men, 'that's where I was raised. I left many years ago when my father made an apprentice agreement with the old Mr Spandler.' Mr Gough was the oldest man employed by Spandler's and he nodded respectfully at Robert.

'I remember when you came, Johnny,' Robert smiled at Mr Gough, 'you were the only apprentice who was not part of the family in those days – and I'm ashamed to say that us three brothers didn't always treat you well.'

'You teased me, as I remember, but it was all in fun – and I've lived comfortably in your employ.' The train had gathered speed again but within a few minutes was slowing down.

'Johnny, you can alight here if you wish and re-join us later. We'll be on the train which leaves Norwich at eleven.' Mr Gough shook his head.

'I've been excited at coming to Norwich – I've not been for many years – so I'll come with you today. Now I know that the trains stop here,' he explained, 'I can come back on my own. If I found some of my folks I would want to stay longer.' He craned his neck this way and that as the train came to a halt.

'Where else does the train stop?' someone else asked.

'I enquired when I bought the tickets,' explained Robert, 'Buckenham, Brundall and then Brandon Junction, where the line divides. Apparently, you'll eventually be able to board a train in Yarmouth and alight in London six and a half hours later.'

'Do you mean you'll be able to reach London on the same day as you leave Yarmouth?' Freddie asked. When he tried to raise his eyebrows to show his astonishment his scars made him look like a frightened rabbit. Everyone laughed and he shrugged. Ten minutes later they could see the spire of Norwich cathedral and the train began to slow down.

'Are we stopping again?'

'No,' said Robert, 'I think we must be at the bridges at Thorpe.' The train clanged as it went over the first of two iron bridges. They were travelling very slowly and the men exclaimed as they saw the river beneath them.

'I don't like this,' squawked Edmund. 'This is a big, heavy train. The bridge will collapse.'

'There are two because we cross over a loop in the river,' said Robert. Many men could be seen accompanied by the sound of pick-axes and shovels. 'It looks like they're digging a new cut for the river. These bridges were built low, for strength, so many ships will no longer be able to reach Norwich.'

'I wonder if there'll be as much trade on the river now,' commented James. 'We've already seen fish being unloaded. The trains will move goods more quickly.'

'That's true.' Robert looked around and raised his voice. 'We're arriving at Norwich now. There is no need for us to stay together but we're travelling back on the eleven o'clock train so you only have an hour and a quarter.' As the train drew to a halt the guard walked along the length calling out, 'All change!' as he unlocked the doors.

There had been those who had declared that they would never travel on the train and a few persisted with their view that travelling so quickly was unhealthy; however, those who tried it said that it was marvellous. The third-class fares were so low that all except the destitute used the train.

'The visitors are all making their way back to the station for the last train to Norwich,' said Henry as he came in from the yard later that summer.

'It was very busy at the market this morning,' replied Mary-Ann, 'although I think the traders are happy. Greensome's have made their stall half as long again and they had a chain of people passing produce from the nursery to the stall, just to keep it stocked.'

'It'll make the town more prosperous. Mind there was trouble at Holkham Tavern – too much ale and too much sun I think. But it will be good for our children. When they're older there'll be plenty of work in the town.' Their eyes met and Henry looked down to Mary-Ann's belly. He gently patted it. 'All's well in there?'

Mary-Ann laughed. 'Yes, though I'm getting near my time so I'd like you to fetch my Ma. The babe could come more quickly while this is my third.'

'I can hear the baby crying,' said Rachel, Henry's sister, to the three girls who were with her outside the door of Francis Buildings. It was the evening of the first Sunday in September.

'I can remember when you were a baby, Martha-Ann,' said Maria, one of the other girls whilst Martha-Ann jumped up and down.

'Come on, let's go in!' she urged. Rachel knocked and opened the door.

'Hello,' she called and heard Mary-Ann call back. She led the girls into the living room where Mary-Ann was sitting in her chair feeding the baby.

'Hello, it's nice to have some visitors, although I think that perhaps it's not really me you've come to see.' Mary-Ann beamed at the girls as she put her finger between the baby's mouth and her nipple to break the suction. 'He's not really sucking properly now, just holding on, so you can pass him round if you want.' Rachel reached out and took him.

'You've called him Henry like his father?' she asked. Mary-Ann nodded.

'Henry's delighted that he's a boy. He is Henry but we're going to call him Harry. It'll stop them both claiming that it wasn't them I wanted when there's a job to be done in years to come.' They laughed.

'We're talking about Henry but he's not here and neither is Tom,' said Rachel.

'That's because they've gone to take my mother back to the farm. It's the busy time of the year and she was wanting to be back. They've taken Louisa and Carrie with them.' Mary-Ann turned to one of the girls.

'Now I know you're Martha, my Henry's youngest sister – and you two must be sisters,' she said turning to the other girls, 'but I cannot yet recall everyone from the family.'

'I'm Maria and this is Martha-Ann,' said the elder of the two girls. 'Our father is Robert.'

'I'm seven,' said the little girl. Mary-Ann smiled at her.

'So who's the older of you two?' She looked from Martha to Maria.

'I am, by two years,' Maria replied.

'I'm twelve,' said Martha, 'and I've been living at Uncle Robert's since I was five so, although they're my cousins, Maria and Martha-Ann are like my sisters. I know that Henry is my brother because Rachel has told me but I don't remember.'

'He often talks about you. He's watched you growing up and is pleased at how you've grown into such a lovely young lady,' Mary-Ann informed her. Martha's face went red and Martha-Ann giggled.

'Would you like me to make you some tea?' Rachel asked as she handed Harry to Maria.

'Oh, yes I would, please. Feeding him always makes me thirsty. You'll need to move the pot from the fire first but be careful – it will be heavy. Mutton stew – my Ma put it on before she left and she said she's done enough for two days. Build the fire up a bit or the kettle'll never boil!'

On the bench Martha and Martha-Ann were sitting either side of Maria. Martha-Ann had found a tiny hand and Harry was grasping her finger. Martha stroked his head. The girls were fascinated by the baby: he epitomised their future.

'Put him in his cradle,' said Mary-Ann, later, to Martha, who was the last of the girls to hold him and in whose arms he had fallen asleep. Maria looked around the room

'My Ma said that we were to help with any cleaning you had before we left,' she said, 'but there's not even any soot round the fireplace.

'That's because my Ma was up early this morning, cleaning like the devil was after her,' Mary-Ann said, 'so there's nothing for you to do – but if you want to come back next weekend!' She winked at the girls and chuckled. They all giggled.

'We'll do that, Mary-Ann, and then you know that you can take some ease this week,' said Maria. The other girls nodded. 'I don't work on Fridays because Grout's couldn't take me on full time so I'll call in then and see if you need anything fetching.'

'Can we hold Harry when we come again?' asked Martha-Ann.

'Of course. I'll look forward to seeing you and so will he!'

Later Henry and Tom returned from taking Abigail home.

'We fixed your Ma and Pa's roof while we were there – they had a leak.' Mary-Ann tutted.

'That farmer, he never does anything for them. I'm sure if the house fell down he'd expect them to sleep in the field. It's just as well you had tools with you.'

'Yes, I take them every time I go because there's always something. I noticed that they both use that support I put in by the front door. It's good to feel that I'm helping them. Have you been alright here while we've been gone?'

'I've had visitors,' Mary-Ann said, 'Rachel and Martha with Maria and Martha-Ann.' Tom laughed.

'You mean Harry had visitors,' he suggested.

'Yes, they did enjoy holding him but they also offered to do some cleaning – and when they saw that Ma had done it all they said they would come back next week.'

'They're good girls,' said Henry, 'like I'd expect Spandler women to be. Caring and not afraid of hard work!' Harry, in his cradle, stirred and started to make small sounds. Henry picked him up: he was moving his head from side to side and opening his mouth.

'Henry, son of Henry, son of Henry, son of Thomas,' he said to him, 'I'd like to think you will be a millwright when you grow up,' His eyes moved over his son's face. Then he looked at Tom and shrugged, 'that's if there is a millwrights' yard for you to work in by then – if Ed's not ruined it.' Harry's movements became more frantic and he started to whimper.

'He needs to feed, Henry, here let me have him,' said Mary-Ann. Henry stared intently at his son's face for a few more moments before passing him over. 'Are there problems at the yard then?' Mary-Ann asked.

'It's just Ed, wanting to make decisions – and Uncle Robert letting him. Insisted that we didn't need to send men to Flowers' mill the other day even though he'd noticed a split in a cog and stopped his mill before it could do any more damage. Said to tell him to continue using it anyway and besides that he said it didn't matter because Mr Flowers had two mills. When Tom said that it would cause more damage if he continued using it Ed told him to be quiet because he was only an apprentice – then his father told him that Tom was right and do you know what he said?' Henry had been speaking rapidly but now he paused. He continued before anyone could reply, 'he said that it would be good if it caused further damage because that would mean more work for us and we'd be able to charge him more – and Mr Flowers is one of our best customers!'

'Perhaps it's for the good Henry,' suggested Tom. Henry snorted. 'No, think about it,' continued Tom, 'if Robert sees him making poor decisions he may realise how inept he is.'

'That's the trouble,' replied Henry, 'I'm sure Robert knows he's inadequate but he's his son and he doesn't want to admit it. Besides which, there's Aunt Mary who takes Edmund's side every time and has no understanding of his faults. Now I know it will be years before Edmund takes over, but…'

'Today we have one of Ma's stews on the fire,' interrupted Mary-Ann, 'and just before you arrived I added some dumplings which should be ready by the time Harry has had his fill which is also just enough time for you two to wash.' She looked at the two men who laughed and went out to the back yard.

During that winter Maria came to Francis Buildings on most Friday afternoons and she and Mary-Ann became good friends. The two Marthas, being younger, were at school but often, on a Sunday afternoon, Maria returned with them. Mary-Ann enjoyed their company. Their conversations were frequently about school and Mary-Ann, having spent her childhood working on the farm, found the glimpse into their childhood fascinating. She also enjoyed hearing about things which were happening in Yarmouth.

'Have you seen, the circus is coming to town in May?' asked Martha one Sunday afternoon after Easter.

'Yes,' Martha-Ann giggled, 'and the clown is going on the river!'

'What ever do you mean?'

'He's going on the river in a wash-tub!' Martha-Ann repeated. Mary-Ann frowned as she tried to understand.

'There's been posters put up,' explained Martha. 'The clown is going to sit in a wash-tub and be pulled up the river by four swans.'

'Seems a rather foolish thing to do,' suggested Mary-Ann.

'Yes, but it will be fun to watch,' replied Martha.

'Apparently he's starting at the drawbridge on the quay and finishing after the suspension bridge,' Maria informed her, 'and I would think that most of the town will come out to watch. I'm sure Louisa would find it amusing.'

'Perhaps but I'll see what Henry says about it and then decide.'

The front door opened and Henry and Tom walked in.

'We found plenty of driftwood so our store is now full,' said Tom, 'it must have been that storm last week.'

'Yes, there were many people out gathering. Someone said two boats were wrecked further up the coast. I hope nobody lost their life but I'm glad of the wood.'

'The girls were telling me about the clown on the river,' said Mary-Ann. Henry raised his eyes to the ceiling.

'It'll be entertaining I suppose,' he said, 'so long as the fool doesn't drown himself, though there'll be plenty of seamen on the ships to pull him out!'

8

'Shall we stay and watch from here?' Mary-Ann asked.

'We're on the bend in the river so we'll have a good view as he swings round. Should be quite funny if he capsizes – I just hope he can swim!' Henry laughed. 'It's coming to rain now. Let's shelter near that house. People may come and stand in front of us but we should still be able to see.'

'Look you can see the bridge from here. A Norwich train must have just come in – look at all the people coming into town!' exclaimed Mary-Ann.

'There must be hundreds of them,' said Maria.

'Yes,' replied Mary-Ann, 'keep holding onto the little ones. We don't want them getting lost in the crowd.' Maria, Martha and Martha-Ann were there and Louisa and Carrie were jumping up and down in excitement beside them. 'I'm going to get some fish before this rain puts his fire out.' She nodded in the direction of one of the fish sellers who was cooking fish on a small fire. Martha-Ann turned to her older sister, Maria, and holding onto both her hands, jumped up and down as fast and high as she could go. Louisa watched for a moment and then took hold of Martha's hands and copied her. Carrie reached up and tugged at her father's arms.

'Me Pa, me do it!' she called to him. Henry held her hands and lifted her up higher than the other two girls every time she jumped. They all laughed.

'Here we are,' said Mary-Ann as she returned, 'He's pulled out the worst of the bones when he gutted it for me but, still, can you keep an eye on Louisa, Maria? She's usually quite good at avoiding the bones. I'll shred it with my fingers for Carrie, that way I should be able to feel them.'

'Is Harry alright?' asked Martha. She peered into the folds of Mary-Ann's coat where he was tied to her.

'He's fast asleep, though he's getting quite heavy to carry like this.'

During the next half hour, while they waited and ate their fish, many people came and crowded the shore with them. Out of their sight, round the bend of the river, a band played. They heard it stop and then the trumpets sounded a fan-fare.

'It's started!' someone in the crowd shouted. People surged forward to see and Henry lifted Louisa and Carrie up onto his shoulders. They giggled.

'There he is!' someone else shouted.

'Look girls, can you see him?' Mary-Ann said as she pointed towards the clown. He was hanging onto the washtub as it spun round in the whirling water. Henry laughed.

'He'll be lucky to make it to the bridge without getting a soaking.' Older children ran along the bank following him and Maria, Martha and Martha-Ann joined them. Henry tried to follow them with the girls on his shoulders but he couldn't keep up and soon turned back.

'He's almost at the bridge now,' called Mary-Ann as he approached. Henry turned around to look.

'My God! Look at the bridge – the roadway is flat.'

'Isn't it always like that?' Mary-Ann was puzzled.

'No, usually the pull of the chains causes it to arc upwards in the middle. But look, there's so many people on the bridge the weight has pushed it flat.' He looked up. 'Those chains must be under a great tension.' He lifted Louisa and Carrie down and just at that moment there was a loud crack. He rushed forward towards the bridge.

'Get off the bridge,' he shouted, 'get off the bridge!' A few people, having heard the noise and felt the bridge judder, started to move. 'Run,' Henry shouted. Some moved nearer the edge to take up the places left by those who had gone; a child sat down between the railings next to all the other children that were there whilst their parents smiled. 'No,' shouted Henry again, terror giving his voice extra volume. For several minutes Henry ran around shouting at people to get off the bridge. Some looked at him as if he'd turned into a madman but the driver of a cart drew back his horses and did not attempt to cross. Then the real madness began as the edge of the bridge nearest to the clown moved down towards the water, slowly at first, giving a few the opportunity of escape. Then it suddenly gathered speed and within a moment the roadway of the bridge became a vertical wall and all upon it tumbled into the water so that those who had been furthest from the edge fell upon those who had been nearer and pushed them down under the water. The cacophony of screams caused Louisa to clap her hands to her ears whilst she stared at Henry and Mary-Ann. Then, very quickly, quietness descended; water slapped on the new wall, which barred its way, and bubbled, as trapped air fought to the surface. Those on the banks stood still for several moments, their eyes seeing what their brains could not fathom, until survivors began to shout stirring them to action.

'Take the girls and go home,' Henry barked at Mary-Ann. She set off up the hill while he turned back to the river. Some men were already in the water where Bessey's Wharf sloped down into the river. Henry waded in up to his knees and one man passed him a small body. He shuddered: it looked to be a young boy but part of his face was missing where it had been swiped by someone's boot; blood oozed from the wound and his arms and legs flopped around as Henry took him. He turned and walked out of the water. On the bank others took the body and he turned back. Seeing the water swirling round his legs he shuddered again: had he anticipated this day when he stood on that bridge, the day Mr Cray had asked about the extension?

Half an hour passed whilst Henry lost count of the bodies. He staggered out of the water with another: a man this time and he was heavy.

'Henry, there you are,' called Thomas, 'the girls are missing.' Henry stood, uncomprehending, for a moment thinking he meant Louisa and Carrie whom he had sent home with Mary-Ann. 'Our Martha, with Maria and Martha-Ann –

they've not come home and we can't find them.' Henry's eyes widened and he went to come with them but Robert stopped him.

'They may be amongst these unfortunate souls you're pulling out. We'll look elsewhere and come back to you if, or when,' he managed a weak smile, 'we find them.'

It was dark by the time Henry returned home. After he entered the door to his house he stopped still while his eyes moved over his family: Mary-Ann who had stood to find him some food when she'd heard him at the door; Caroline and Henry in the pen and Louisa sitting at the table looking at a book from school. He went first to Mary-Ann and hugged her then picked up each of the children in turn and stared into their faces. Henry wriggled to be put down again. Caroline smiled at him although he did not return her smile. Louisa frowned and stroked his face.

'We're safe, Pa,' she whispered. Tears started to run down his face and he kept brushing them away. At six years of age she had some understanding of what had happened.

'Sit down with her,' suggested Mary-Ann, 'while I make you a drink.' Henry nodded and flopped down into the chair. He was shaking and Louisa held his hands.

'Don't cry, Pa. It's alright. No-one's hurt.' Henry hugged her and the force of it caused her eyes to open wide as she looked towards her mother. He looked over to the pen as more tears blurred his vision. Mary-Ann returned with a tankard of tea.

'Drink this while I put the children in bed. I kept them up because I thought you would need to see them.' Henry looked at her, his gaze following her about the room as she picked up Henry, balanced Caroline on her hip and walked behind Louisa through the door to the stairs. He was still staring at the door when she returned.

' "No-one's hurt," she said. I wish I could only know what she knows,' said Henry. He sniffed. 'I lost count of the number of bodies that were pulled out of the water. Must have been at least twenty-five and that was just what I could see near where I was standing. There'll be others further along the bank and over the river.'

'Were they all,' she paused, 'dead.' He shook his head.

'Some coughed and others were sick or groaned or moved – and there were others with broken arms and legs. Then there was a child – I don't know how they'll find out who he was because his face was missing. I could see the marks of someone's boot on his flesh.' The words tumbled out of him. He shuddered and the tears flowed again. Mary-Ann held him tight. She did not speak for a long time.

'Louisa's right though, we're all here and safe, thanks to you and your caution. If we'd gone on the bridge like I'd wanted to...' At this he gripped her tighter. Then he suddenly pulled away.

'Has Thomas not returned?' Mary-Ann shook her head. 'Robert?' Mary-Ann's frown deepened while she shook her head again.

'The girls are missing,' Henry explained, 'they said they'd come back to me if they found them. I must go to the yard and see.'

'The girls!' Mary-Ann clapped her hand to her mouth. 'You mean Maria...' Her voice faltered as Henry picked up his coat and moved to the door with huge strides. He turned back to her.

'Martha – I sent her away to keep her safe when she was small. I hope they've found her, found them all.' Then he was gone and Mary-Ann fell back into her chair, her eyes wide as she stared into the fire.

When Henry reached the yard he went straight to the cottage and through the empty office. At the parlour door he stopped suddenly and reeled backwards. On the table was a body, covered by a sheet. He looked across the room to where Robert was standing.

'Who?' His voice cracked.

'Maria,' Robert's voice was strangely hard. 'I told them not to go on the bridge. The two Marthas were pulled from the water. Thomas is taking them to James and Hannah. My Mary cannot give them the care they need – she collapsed when we brought Maria home.' He nodded towards the table. 'Mary's upstairs in bed and my sister Hannah is looking after her.' Henry held Robert's shoulders and, as the older man began to sob, he hugged him. But then Robert stopped, drew a deep breath and continued, 'but you need to go and see Martha – she's hurt.' Henry saw the grief and fear in the older man's eyes whilst his own heart froze within him.

He was breathless when he arrived at the house of James and Hannah. His uncle answered the door and he did not smile but turned around and led Henry upstairs. Hannah looked up as the men entered.

'Martha-Ann's asleep.' She nodded over the corner of the room. 'She was just wet and cold. But I'm worried about Martha.' She turned back to the bed next to which she stood. Martha was lying on her back, her eyes wide open. There was a graze on her right cheek around which the blood had congealed and her left arm was covered in bloody bandages.

'They were taken to one of the houses by the river,' James explained, 'Martha-Ann told us before she went to sleep. They were put on a blanket in the corner of the room and there were lots of other people. Some were crying but most were still and quiet, like Maria. Then a doctor came and she told them where they were from. The doctor ordered Martha's arm to be bandaged and they were carried to the yard. Thomas and I brought these two here. Mary was overcome.'

'I think, once Martha-Ann's had a good night's sleep, she'll be fine,' said Hannah, 'I'm sure Robert and Mary will be glad to have her home tomorrow. I'll look after Martha, unless you want to take her home?' Henry shook his head.

'She knows you better than my Mary-Ann.' Henry replied. 'Her arm seems to lie strangely and there's a great deal of bandage on it – do you know what it's like underneath?'

'Martha-Ann said she screamed when they were bandaging it and there was something sticking out of her arm. Bone probably.' She met Henry's eyes and her look conveyed her anxiety.

'She is young and strong and she has a good nurse. If my Mary-Ann knows of any of her plants that will help she'll come with them – but for now I must go back to her and let her know what's happened. She's going to take it hard. Maria has become a good friend these last eight months.'

That day Mr Gough, the oldest worker at the yard, had travelled on the train to the village of Cantley where he'd been raised so that knew nothing of the horror which had struck the town until he returned. Then he found that his eldest daughter with her youngest child had been on the bridge and were still missing. The following day, at the yard, James was in charge: the door to the cottage was firmly closed and Robert was not to be seen. As Mr Gough rounded the corner from the passage which led from the street, James saw him and immediately crossed the yard to him.

'I-I'm sorry I'm late,' Mr Gough stuttered as he removed his cap.

'I understand,' James replied, 'the other men have told me. Have you found...' Mr Gough shook his head. 'Do you want to go and keep on looking?'

'I - er - I...,' Mr Gough's eyes travelled over James's face. James smiled and put a hand on his shoulder.

'We will still pay you. In all the years you've worked here we've never known you take time off, or even arrive late. Take some time – Robert is.' James nodded towards the cottage.

'I heard about the young girl. I'm so sorry, and thank you,' said Mr Gough. He replaced his cap and turned to leave the yard. As he approached the passage Henry appeared. Mr

Gough doffed his cap but he passed Henry without a word. Henry looked at James.

'He has family who are still missing,' James explained, 'I've sent him home.' Henry nodded. 'What of you? Do you want to go to Martha?'

'No. Aunt Hannah is looking after her. What could I do but sit and watch? I'd rather be here.'

'Martha moaned a lot in the night but I think most of it was in her sleep. Hannah gave her laudanum. We sent a message for the doctor to call but many people will want him today.' Henry shuddered as he remembered the young boy: if he was still alive he would certainly need help.

'When we stop for bread I will go and see her. Perhaps he will have been by then and I can find out more.'

'Hannah is worried. She says she thinks that the doctor will want to take off the arm.' Henry startled and shuddered again.

'Of course, I remember, when I was a child – Mr Grant the carter – they took his leg off. I remember my Pa saying that his bone was sticking through his skin. But Martha, well, she's a young girl!'

At midday, when Henry and James arrived, the doctor was there. He had his hand on Martha's forehead and was looking intently at her arm. He had not removed the bandages. He looked up as they entered.

'She is hot,' he stated, 'and look at her arm.' Henry frowned: he knew her arm was damaged. However when he looked closer he could see streaks of red in her flesh coming from underneath the bandage. The doctor continued, 'we need to amputate.'

'Take her arm off? But..'

'You have no choice unless you want to watch her die. When that red reaches her heart, it will kill her. If we take the arm off above the redness we could save her but it may have advanced too far already. Certainly, by tomorrow there will be no hope in trying and she will be dead by the end of the week, if not sooner.' Henry looked at twelve-year-old Martha. Tears flooded her face but she made no sound. He stroked her head.

'What do you want to do?'

'I don't want to die.'

'Taking your arm off will hurt more than you can imagine – some people die with shock,' said the doctor. 'First the surgeon will cut round your arm and then he will use a large saw to cut through your bone and after all that you may die anyway.'

'How long will it take?' Martha's voice was very quiet.

'As short a time as he can do it. Less than a minute. If you faint with the first cut it will be quicker because you won't be able to struggle.'

'Cut off my arm. I want to try to not die.' Henry's eyes misted over as he marvelled at the steadiness of his sister's voice.

'Take her there now,' ordered the doctor. 'There are others to amputate this afternoon but if you bring her as I go now, I will ask the surgeon to do her first before she hears the sounds from the others.' Henry felt the room dim for a moment and held onto the bedstead: there was a coldness and he briefly saw his father's coffin once again. He took a deep breath to steady himself and felt a hand on his shoulder.

'Come, let's take the bedroom door off,' said James, 'we can carry her on that.'

They made a strange procession through the town, Henry and James following behind the doctor with Martha on the door between them. Henry was aware that others being carried on boards, whom they passed on their way, were covered by a shroud. He wondered whether Martha would be likewise covered on their return journey.

'Take your board and wait outside. You will need to take her away again afterwards, one way or the other,' the doctor said after he'd helped them move her onto a table. Henry looked around the room. There were some tiered seats at one end upon which a group of young men were sitting. The surgeon, his apron covered in the bloodstains of many operations, was standing next to him.

'They can join the students and sit and watch – if they have the stomach for it.' He laughed as Henry and James picked up the door.

'She is my sister. I cannot watch you hurt her,' said Henry as he bent down and stroked Martha's head.

'Be gone with you then. Best not delay.' The surgeon busied himself drawing a knife and a saw from his case. Placing the saw on the floor by his feet he steadied the knife in his hand. He did not look at Martha's face but the doctor did. He was holding Martha's arm tightly whilst two of the students hung onto the rest of her body to try and stop her from moving. Henry and James quickly moved back out of the room.

A few moments later Henry eyes opened wide at the sound of the saw. He frowned and looked at James.

'A blessing – she's fainted or we'd hear her screams,' his uncle suggested. The next moment the doctor was by their side.

'You can come and take her home now. She is an amazing young girl. Her eyes grew larger as the surgeon worked but she did not move – and you heard how quiet she was.' They followed the doctor back into the operating theatre. The surgeon was standing by the table and Martha's blood still dripped from his saw; next to him one of the students was bandaging the stump of her arm.

'She was better than any man I've ever cut,' he declared, 'so quiet and still that I thought she'd fainted and wondered if she might be dead. But then, when I'd finished, I looked at her and those big eyes were staring at me.' He bowed in Martha's direction and left the room.

'Do you see that rope around the top of the stump?' asked the doctor. Henry and James nodded. 'When you reach home loosen it but then immediately tie it again. Do that every quarter hour for the next two hours. Then loosen it and watch the bandage. If blood starts to seep through then tie it up again. If it doesn't you can leave it untied – but don't take it off the arm completely for the next few days so that it is ready if it starts to bleed again. Then hope and pray that the redness doesn't return.'

9

The second day after the disaster was a Sunday and the church of St Nicholas was full. The people heard the vicar preach a sermon in which he said that the disaster had been God's wrath falling upon the town. He said that it was wicked that there was no school for the poor of Great Yarmouth and consequently, because of their ignorance, the poor did not come to worship and had made God angry. He declared that the town should raise money to restore the church and build a Priory School as a propitiation for their sins.

'I don't agree with him,' declared Mary-Ann that evening. 'The reason poor don't come to church is because they have to stand – they cannot afford the pew rent.'

'Yes, but how many are there who, although poor, spend much of their time and money in the ale house,' countered Tom, 'but if they stayed sober at home they could afford the pew rent. It is only a few pennies.'

'Yes, and the rich can have the ale and still sit down in church. A tankard of ale is one of the few pleasures a poor man can afford.' Mary-Ann's eyes flashed and Tom was silenced.

On his way to work the following day Henry went to see Martha and was rewarded with a small smile.

'I keep forgetting it's gone until I look down and it's not there. He cut it off just above my elbow,' she said, 'but sometimes it's as if I can still feel my fingers.'

'That's strange. Is it sore, where he cut it off?' Martha's eyes closed for a moment. 'I'm sorry, I didn't mean to remind you.'

'It is, but not nearly as much as it hurt before. I realised it felt better as you were carrying me home. On the way there it hurt really badly.'

'It's good to hear you talking more so you must be feeling a little recovered.' Henry walked to the door of the bedroom. 'I'll come back and see you again on my way home. I'm so proud of you – my courageous sister.'

'I'm going to the yard now – but you stay with her if you want,' James called from the foot of the stairs.

'No, I'm coming now.' He turned and smiled back at Martha before following his uncle out of the house.

'It seems to have worked,' said James as they walked to the yard.

'I hope so. It appears to have stopped bleeding. It's wondrous how she bore the pain of the knife – she deserves to recover.'

They'd reached the yard and Henry had his hand on the door when they heard a bell ringing. The town crier was out so they walked on past the churchyard into the Market Square to listen.

'Hear this!' he shouted. 'Bring the bodies of those who have died to the Town Hall.'

'Let's go to the Angel and see what is on the notice,' suggested James. 'Robert will want to know.'

'On Tuesday the sixth day of May the bodies of the victims of the disaster, with each family walking alongside their deceased, will be taken in procession from the Town Hall to St Nicholas's,' Henry read.

'Dus't mean there'll be just one service for all t'folks who died?' asked a man standing next to them. Henry moved to let him see but the man shrugged 'Can't read. Tell me.'

'The townsfolk of Great Yarmouth will stand as the procession goes by. The funeral service will be read over each departed soul on as many afternoons as necessary.'

'I shink m'missus be at peace wiv'at,' he wiped his brow which caused him to be unsteady. Henry could smell the alcohol on the man's breath. He put his hand on his shoulder.

'Take yourself home to her,' he said, 'for she'll need you now.' The man left.

'We must go to the yard,' said James.

'I think I'd rather keep Maria here and we'll bury her as a family on another day,' said Robert when they told him. 'I can't see that the vicar will say each one separately. He might start out like that...' Robert voice faltered.

'Apparently the vicar is going to have help,' explained Henry, 'and there will be five other clerics as well. The notice definitely says they are going to say the full service over each and that each and every person will have their own committal. It looks like the whole town will mourn with you.'

'I'm not sure what Mary will say,' Robert hesitated.

'It will be an occasion that will be remembered for generations,' James pointed out. Robert looked at him as he continued, 'and because of that I think that it would be good if you took your place.' Robert's head fell forward and his shoulders drooped.

'M-m-my M-Maria. She was nearly a w-woman,' he sobbed and his breath came in gulps. James led him from the yard into the cottage. Henry stood alone, staring, unseeing, until James returned.

'It's hard for them both,' he said to Henry, 'but Mary said she would draw comfort from the prayers of the rest of the town. They will take Maria to the Town Hall shortly. It just happens that young Robert's ship is here this week, so he and his father will take her.' He approached the other men who were working. 'Let us stand on either side between the cottage and the yard door as they come out.' The men stopped their work and formed a solemn guard as Robert, with his two elder sons Robert and Edmund, carried Maria's coffin from the cottage.

An hour later, the midday bread had arrived from Boulter's, and the men had just put down their tools when they looked up at the sound of the yard gate. It was Mr Gough and at the sight of his face smiles broke out between them.

'My Sally were on t'Cobham side of the bridge and she and her babe were pulled out the water. Vauxhall Inn gave them shelter but I must return with some money.'

'It's good to have something to smile about,' one of the men commented as the others murmured their agreement. 'So, someone pulled her out?'

'Yes, she held t'child's clothes with her teeth and paddled herself t'bank. She doesn't know how t'swim but she said she knew she had to do it t'save herself and young Alf. People saw her, pulled her out and took her t'Inn.'

'How did you find her?'

'Well yesterday we'd looked in all t'Inns and Taverns where people were taken on this side of t'river so this morning we went looking for a way across. Found a young boy with a rowing boat. I was cross at first when he told me it would be tuppence t'go across and then if there were others coming back t'would be more.'

'Tut,' said James, 'making money from people's misery.' Mr Gough shook his head.

'That's what I said to him and he began to cry. His Pa is a fisherman and away at sea. His Ma usually took in washing to earn pennies with which to feed t'family while he was away but she and had drowned with two others. There were three other children, all younger than he, and he needed t'pennies to feed them 'til his Pa returned – so I gladly paid him his pennies and Mrs Gough has taken food round to him this morning.' The other men nodded.

'There are many families ruined by this,' said one of them. 'It's good that yours is not one of them.' There was silence for a moment or two.

'They took Mr Spandler's girl to the town hall this morning,' said James quietly. Mr Gough nodded.

'He grieves while my family is saved. Calamities happen t'master and worker alike.'

When Henry returned to James's house that evening he could tell that Martha was in more pain than she'd been in the morning. Her cheeks were flushed and her smile was gone. He returned home to Mary-Ann.

'She was saying that she feels hot again, like she did before and it's hurting more.' Mary-Ann was quiet for a few moments.

'I'm sorry but I think it's going bad again. The red streaks will return,' she said. 'I've seen it before – one of the other children on the farm – it was just his finger but it went red again.'

'What shall we do? She will die.'

'My Ma – she put something on it,' Mary-Ann frowned, 'but I can't remember. Something in the bandage.'

In the middle of the night Mary-Ann suddenly sat up in bed.

'Bread. Stale bread,' she said aloud.

'Huh, what?' Henry mumbled.

'Stale bread, that's what she used in the bandage. Every time she changed the bandage the bread was full of the poison.' Henry, wide awake now, gripped Mary-Ann tightly.

'Tomorrow, go and see Aunt Hannah tomorrow and show her as soon as you can.'

'No, I must go now. The poison may spread very quickly. Come with me – it has to be now,' Mary-Ann insisted. She went downstairs and looked in the bottom of the box where they kept their bread, removing a few stale crusts. She looked at the loaf she had and cut off some from the end. 'I've left enough for the morning.,' she whispered to Henry after they'd donned some clothes and found their cloaks. 'Have you told Thomas that we're going?' Henry nodded. 'Come on, let's go.'

As they approached James's house they could see that there was a light on already and Henry knew that it was in the room where Martha was. James, his face tight and drawn, led them upstairs. Martha was moaning and her legs kept kicking up into the air so that she looked as if she was trying to run up an imaginary wall. Her eyes were staring at the ceiling and sweat was pouring down her face. Hannah was wiping her forehead and talking quietly to her. She turned as they entered.

'I don't even know if she can hear me,' she said. Henry's eyes went to Martha's arm. Underneath the bandage where it covered the stump he could see a redness and it was forming lines towards the top of her arm. The stench made him retch.

'There's no time to be lost,' said Mary-Ann. She unwrapped the bundle and out fell the bread. Hannah looked at her and shook her head.

'She cannot eat. Can't you see?'

'No,' said Mary-Ann, 'not for her to eat. To put in the bandage. Take it off.' Henry turned away as the raw flesh on the end of Maria's stump was exposed. Mary-Ann wiped the oozing mess with the ends of the old bandage and then put the stale pieces of bread on the wound before wrapping new bandages round it. 'The bread will draw the poison to itself. At about midday tomorrow undo it again, take the old bread away and put more on it. I've brought the end of the loaf I had. If you leave it out it should be stale enough to use by then – it needs to be dry for it to work. You should find that the poison is all in the bread. You'll be able to re-use the bandage.'

'That's good,' said Hannah, 'I'm running short of cloth to cut up.'

When they left nothing seemed to have changed: Maria hadn't shown any signs of knowing that they'd been there at all; her legs continued their frenzied movement and she was still hot and staring at the ceiling.

'If it's going to work, there should be an improvement during the day,' said Mary-Ann as they walked home. Looking beyond Southtown across the marshes they could see light beginning to creep into the sky. Henry did not reply.

When he woke again a few hours later he could not bear to take himself to James's house but went straight to the yard. When the church clock started tolling James instructed them all to stop working and to go and stand by the procession. They stood on Church Plain and watched as the long line of bodies snaked across the Market Square from the end of Regent Street up which they'd come from the Town Hall. Some were in coffins but many were just wrapped in shrouds and carried on wooden boards. Henry felt a wave of grief surge over him as they approached. Many families carried more than one corpse. There was one group that, as they walked along, brought expressions of even deeper horror to faces of the townsfolk who lined the route because they appeared to be merely the remnants of a family: two men, one of them elderly, carried the body of an adult and they were followed by three youths with two more small bodies between them and a young girl, the only female, who carried a baby. People looked at her but whenever anyone caught her eye she shook her head: the baby was also dead. They watched as Maria's coffin was taken into the church: her funeral service would not be until the following day. By the time the last one had passed it was six o'clock and James instructed them all to go to their homes. He walked alongside Henry.

'My Hannah said she thought Martha was a little calmer this morning when I was leaving. Are you coming back with me now?' Henry hesitated before nodding.

'I dread what I will find. I do not understand what my Mary-Ann did last night. How can stale bread take away the poison?' He shrugged, 'but then her mother knows much about healing and otherwise we would just watch Martha die without trying anything.'

When they arrived Henry climbed the stairs to the room with a heavy heart. As he entered he let out the breath he didn't know he'd been holding. Martha was still: the manic kicking had stopped.

'She is quiet,' said Hannah from the chair where she was sitting. 'Sleeping – after last night she must be exhausted. When I replaced the bread it was heavy with pus. By then she was still but watched me with wide-open eyes. After I'd finished she fell asleep.' She stood up and walked over to Martha. 'Look, you can see that it's still red but I'm sure the lines are shorter.' Henry nodded and smiled for the first time that day.

'She was sleeping quietly,' Henry said to Mary-Ann when he arrived home, 'so it seems to be working.'

'I'm pleased she's more restful but prepare yourself because she's not out of danger. The poison might start coming more quickly than the bread can take it away.'

The following morning Henry entered St Nicholas's church but he was unprepared for what he saw: row after row of the dead lay on the floor in the south aisle and it was clear that most of them were not big enough to be adults. His chest became tight and he bit his lip as he dug his finger nails into his palms. He took his place in the Spandler pews behind Robert, Mary and their children. He bowed his head for a moment and when he looked up James, with his sons James and Freddie, had joined him. During the service for Maria, Henry noticed that Edmund, tears clearly visible on his face, was leaning on his older brother Robert. Robert, their father, looked at them occasionally but his face was impassive. When all the services had been said for that day's burials, the families moved forward to carry their bodies to the graveyard and, forming another procession led by the clergy, made their way out of the south door of the church. A pit had been dug and in it was a large wooden crate for the corpses of those families could not afford a coffin. The Spandler family stood with Maria's coffin on the ground between them, whilst each person was committed to the grave and lowered into the box. There were three bodies, whose families, like the Spandlers, had provided a coffin for them: Maria's had been made in the family millwrights' yard, by her father and older brothers. The procession moved to other parts of the graveyard where three more graves had been dug. Henry noticed that there was a group of townsfolk who had been in the church and stayed for the committals: some stood reverentially in support of those who grieved but he was dismayed by part of the group who were talking and pointing and even sometimes laughing.

'Edmund was very upset,' Henry commented to James as they made their way back to the yard.

'He blames himself. Apparently, he says that he was talking with Maria last week. She'd told him she'd been to collect a parcel from the station for Robert who'd told her to cross the bridge quickly and not loiter on it whereupon Edmund had laughed and told her we were a group of old men who were frightened by the new technology. Told her to wait until he was in charge of the yard and then see the advancements it would embrace and, of course, he also told her that the bridge was safer now the new footpaths had been added to the sides. He thinks that if he'd not had that conversation with her then maybe she wouldn't have gone on the bridge.'

'Perhaps he will learn from this then.'

'The trouble is that he can't learn how to think.' James sighed. 'You remember he was my apprentice. I tried hard to teach him because I could see how important it was to Robert but he just seemed unable to understand. When I'd talk to him about weights and forces and angles and suchlike his eyes would glaze over as if I was talking another language like one of the foreign hands from the ships on the quay. I would ask him a question and he'd just shake his head – well sometimes he'd try and answer but it was clear that he didn't know what he was saying. It's a wonder he wants to stay at the yard. His younger brother, Richard, seems a bright young lad.'

'Yes, but Edmund can only see himself as the master in charge. If he went elsewhere he would have to work his way to importance instead of just inheriting it.' The two men looked at each other and they both shrugged.

'That he would never do,' scoffed James.

'Well I'm sorry he's upset and blames himself. I know only too well how that feels.'

'Do you still blame yourself about the deaths of your father's family?' James's voice expressed his surprise. Henry nodded.

'Well, not so much blame I suppose. It was all very much my father's fault. If he hadn't sold his share and lost it all in London more of my siblings would have grown to adults and my Ma might still be alive – but I do often wonder if I could have done more.' Henry shrugged. 'And now Martha may die.' Henry's mouth was tight and the pitch of his voice had risen.

'You saw her this morning. She seems so much better. My Hannah says you'd never believe how much poison is in the bread each time she changes it.' Henry shook his head.

'Mary-Ann says it could still go badly for her. The poison may increase and be more than the bread can control.'

They arrived at James's house to find Martha sitting up in bed talking with Hannah. She smiled at them as they came in and Henry went straight to her.

'It's good. You're well!'

Martha nodded. 'It seemed strange when your Mary-Ann put the bread on my arm.'

'You knew we were there then?'

'Yes, I could hear you all talking,' she chuckled, 'and I can remember thinking you must wonder if I was going mad with my legs kicking up all the time. Then I thought the bread was odd and perhaps Mary-Ann was the one that was mad!'

'I must go home to Mary-Ann. She will be pleased to know how well you are.' He turned back from the door and Martha waved at him.

'It's good that it was my left hand that was hurt. It would have been hard to have to learn to do things if he'd cut off my right hand.' Henry waved back at her and smiled as he left. It amazed him that Martha could say that it was good that her left hand had been cut off: he knew that, had it been his arm, he would not have managed to see anything good about it at all.

As he walked home he thought of Maria's death and the sadness of Uncle Robert. People passed him on the street but no-one smiled. A weariness overcame him so that it was all that he could do to put one foot in front of the other to reach his home.

In bed that night they held each other. Mary-Ann was sniffing.

'M-Maria's gone. M-My friend. I'm alone again.'

'You have me.' Mary-Ann stopped crying and gave Henry a squeeze.

'Yes, so I'm not really alone but it was good to have another woman to talk to.'

'I miss her as well. I can remember being glad when I heard the two of you laughing together. Was it only last week?'

'Yes.' Mary-Ann continued to hold Henry tightly but she didn't say anything else. Henry did not speak either. They lay in silence for several long minutes.

'I must use the pot again,' Mary-Ann said as she left the bed.

'What again?'

'Yes, actually I think it may be good news. The smell from the Shambles made me retch today when I was at the market and I should have bled last week.'

'You mean?' Henry's voice was excited.

'Usually I wait for a few weeks to tell you so that I'm really sure, but yes, I think I'm with child again,' she replied as she climbed back into bed. Henry hugged her.

'So, amongst all the pain and sorrow we have something to cheer our hearts and those around us. I will tell Robert and James tomorrow.'

10

At the end of the following day Henry and Thomas came home laden with pieces of wood. Mary-Ann frowned in puzzlement.

'You're with child again and it must be quite crowded in your room already so I'm moving back up to the attic,' explained Thomas. 'I'm going to make it more comfortable.'

'I've said I'll help him,' added Henry. 'Apparently when he slept up there before things fell on him in the night.'

'What sort of things?'

'Oh, dirt and spiders and suchlike. It's not knowing what it is when you feel it on your face in the dark that I don't like. I'm going to cover the rafters.' Mary-Ann laughed.

'I would hate you to have your mouth open and swallow a spider,' she called out after them as they went upstairs.

The days passed and the town of Great Yarmouth began to return to normal: music was heard in the taverns again and children were free to run and play without being curtailed by adults. It was Sunday two weeks after the bridge collapse and it was sunny.

'Let's eat and then take a walk by the sea, like we used to. Not really warm enough for the children to play on the sand but it will be good to be in the sunshine,' said Henry as they walked back from church.

'Perhaps Martha will feel like coming with us,' suggested Mary-Ann. 'She could cover her stump with a shawl and if one of us stays on her left we can make sure no-one bumps into her. And maybe Martha-Ann as well. They probably haven't been out since...' Mary-Ann's voice trailed off.

'Robert and Mary and the family weren't at church again this morning.'

'Go back, call in at the yard and see how they are. You could ask about Martha-Ann coming with us at the same time. I'll carry on home and make dinner, then when you come back it'll be ready. We don't know for how long this weather's going to stay sunny.'

Later they made their way down St Nicholas Road. Martha had been hesitant at first but now she was smiling broadly. Mary-Ann, with Harry tied to her, walked next to Martha. Henry was on Martha's other side and she took his arm. In front of them Martha-Ann and Louisa skipped along whilst Carrie tried to keep up with them.

'It makes people laugh, sometimes, having only one arm,' said Martha. She giggled when Henry and Mary-Ann suddenly looked at her. 'No, I don't mean they're being unkind. I can get my food onto my fork quite easily with only one hand until I reach the end. Last night I was chasing the last piece of carrot around my plate and we were all laughing. Then Aunt Hannah put her fork on my plate to stop it moving and I was able to catch it.'

'Sounds like a project for Tom. He could mould you a special plate with a rim that you could use to push against.' Martha grinned.

'That was just what Uncle James said!'

They reached the end of the road and could see the sea. Here the road gave way to coarse grasses which had taken hold in the sand but as they walked towards the sea the grasses thinned out and the ground became soft and difficult to walk on.

'Do you want to walk further, nearer to the sea?' Henry asked. 'I could show you how I make stones bounce on the water.' Martha shook her head.

'I don't think I want to be near to the water at all,' she said. Henry looked at her and then glanced at his wife.

'I think we've walked far enough for your first outing. We should go back,' suggested Mary-Ann. 'We could have toast round the fire.'

'Yes please,' said Martha with a small smile.

'It was good to see Martha so well,' commented Henry later that evening.

'Yes, I enjoyed hearing her stories and she was walking quite strongly. I noticed she was only holding your arm for balance on the way down – but then she went very pale and was leaning on you by the time we got back here. She's been through a lot,' Mary-Ann warned. Henry looked up sharply.

'You mean you think it could still go wrong? She's not out of danger?' Mary-Ann shook her head but then shrugged her shoulders.

'She's young and she's shown how strong she is – others would be dead already – so perhaps I'm worrying without cause. I'll be at ease if she's well at the year's end and I'll be pleased to have been proved a doubter.'

'She's having spasms,' said James a week later, 'grinding her teeth together and squeezing her hand into a tight fist.' They had just left the yard. 'Last night we heard a strange sound and then we realised it was Martha. Her mouth was open but she could only make grunting noises.' They reached James's house and Henry's stomach churned as he climbed the stairs to the room where Martha was. He found her in bed, which she hadn't been when he had visited recently, but she smiled at him as he entered.

'The spasms have stopped for the moment. They've been starting and stopping,' explained Hannah, 'and I don't know what to do. Would your Mary-Ann know?' Henry shrugged his shoulders.

'I won't stay long. Tom should be at home by the time I return. I'll see what Mary-Ann says. I may come straight back with her if she knows. If she doesn't, and it's still happening tomorrow, I think we should bring the doctor back.'

The following day, when Mary-Ann was walking past Owle's the Chemist down by South Quay, she noticed a display in the window. It was for carbolic soap: there were pictures of wounds being washed with it and, because she could not read the words, she entered the shop to find out about it. Five minutes later she left and made her way straight to James and Hannah's house with her purchase.

'The chemist says it's what the surgeons in London are using. They clean wounds with it. Stops there being so much pus,' she explained to Hannah.

'But the stale bread seems to have dealt with the pus. See it's not weeping much now.' Mary-Ann looked at the stump.

'Yes, the bread has done well,' she looked at Martha and smiled, 'I think that maybe you would not be alive if we had not used it. Now I do not know whether this will stop the spasms or not but it cannot harm to try.'

'It w-will hurt though,' Martha cried, 'I'm tired of hurting.' The two women said nothing but Hannah put a small pan of water on the bedroom fire. When it had warmed they poured it into a bowl and made a lather with the soap. Then, as gently as she could, Mary-Ann rubbed it into the flesh at the end of Martha arm. Martha whined, tears rolled down her face and her one hand tightened itself into a fist.

'Look at her feet,' breathed Hannah. Mary-Ann glanced towards them and saw that the toes had curled towards the soles of her feet. Then she picked up the bar of soap again and made fresh lather with it in the water. She turned back to the stump and massaged yet more of it into the wound, forcing it past clots and scabs that had formed. She didn't say anything until she had finished. Then she sat up and stroked Martha's face. She turned to Hannah.

'I think it's the lockjaw. You will need to do as I have done the next few evenings. Leave the wound open to the air when you have finished – just cover it lightly at night.'

Three days later Mary-Ann returned.

'It's not working,' said Hannah, 'in fact the spasms are getting worse. She hasn't eaten since yesterday morning.'

Martha looked from one to the other, her eyes brimming with tears. 'The doctor came yesterday and he suggested we bought some carbolic acid soap and washed it with that. I told him we had already done that.' She turned to directly face Mary-Ann and said in a low voice, 'He said there's nothing more that can be done. She might recover or…'

The following week, when Henry arrived at James's house one morning before work, he found everyone smiling.

'She hasn't had another spasm since yesterday afternoon!' Hannah said, excitement causing her to laugh. Henry clapped his hands together.

'Perhaps you have won,' he said to Martha. 'Martha versus the lockjaw and Martha is the victor!' Martha smiled weakly at him.

'She is very thin, but she can eat again now and must regain her strength,' said Hannah.

'I don't understand why it is taking her such a long time to recover,' said Henry two weeks later. 'That day when we went down to the beach – I know she tired easily and that would have been because she'd been through the horror of having her arm amputated – but she seemed to be better. Now she can't get back from those spasms. Hannah says she needs a lot of encouragement to eat.'

'The lockjaw is exhausting. Try holding your hand in a tight fist and you will find it hurts after a while. Some of her spasms included her feet and even her legs and they went on for a long time. Sometimes they went on most of the night. Then add to that not being able to open or close your mouth so that you can't eat.' Mary-Ann shook her head. 'It would be hard for a strong man, but a young girl…'

'But she stopped having the spasms weeks ago. She's recovered from the lockjaw.'

'It leaves behind it's effect. I fear she may be forever an invalid.'

Midsummer arrived. Although they were still sad from the loss of their daughter, Robert and Mary provided the family feast as usual. All the family came to the yard. Standing with Robert and Mary by the door to the cottage were their children, with the exception of their eldest, Robert, who was back on board his ship. Edmund lurked in the doorway of the cottage and Henry noticed that he was not looking at anyone. Henry's sisters, Mary and Rachel, were standing either side of Martha who was seated and they were next to James and Hannah whose younger children were playing with Louisa and Carrie. Harry was beginning to take his first few steps even though he had not quite reached his first birthday and was trying to keep up with the other children. Jim and Freddie, James and Hannah's older sons, were standing with Henry and Mary-Ann. Sitting together on a bench against the wall near the cottage were two ladies, Elizabeth and Hannah, the widowed sisters of Robert and James. Everyone accepted that there would be no music and dancing that year.

'Look at Harry!' Mary, Henry's sister, called. Mary, Robert wife chuckled and Robert, whose arm she leant on, smiled.

'Reminds me of when Edmund was small,' he said, 'with those podgy legs and falling down every few steps. It's good to hear you laugh,' he said as he patted his wife's hand. Henry, who was watching and listening, didn't know whether to be pleased that Harry was making his aunt and uncle smile or whether to be vexed by the comparison with Edmund.

'I think Edmund was a good deal older than Harry,' advised Mary. She turned to Mary-Ann. 'He's not one year of age yet, is he?' Mary-Ann shook her head and Hannah, James's wife, laughed.

'I seem to remember that Edmund couldn't sit without rolling over at that age. You were quite worried,' she said to Mary.

'That's right. I think he was coming up to three when he was trying to walk and kept falling down.' Henry looked round and saw Edmund sitting by one of the workbenches. He was very interested in the plateful of food he was eating and Henry wondered whether he had heard any of the conversation.

Later in the evening, when all the children had been taken home, Henry returned and spent a pleasant hour talking and supping ale with his uncles.

It was the end of June when Mary-Ann woke with pain in her stomach. It had been happening on and off for the previous few days and she knew what it was. Perhaps she could make it stop again so she lay still for some time, forcing herself not to tense her muscles but to lie still with her abdomen relaxed. Suddenly she felt a wetness between her legs and knew then that it was inevitable. She stumbled from the bed. The first thing Henry saw was Mary-Ann, lit by a ray of morning sunshine, as she crouched on the chamber pot. When she gave a small moan of pain he sat up.

'Are you alright?' Mary-Ann shook her head.

'It's the baby. My body won't carry it any more...' She stopped as another contraction started. She moaned again and Henry came and knelt beside her. She leant on him.

'I am having my bleeding but it is worse than usual because the baby had started to grow. It started a few days ago. I didn't tell you because it kept stopping and sometimes when that happens the baby keeps growing anyway. But it's too much now.' She rose from the bucket and wiped blood from her legs. Henry started to lead her back to the bed. 'Just hold me. I feel quite weak,' she said, 'I want to look in the pot.'

'Ugh,' grunted Henry as he glanced at it, 'it's full of piss and blood. Why do you want to look in there?'

'Because I want to be sure that it has really left me. If it hasn't I might not recover well. My Ma knows some plants that will expel it.'

'What – expel our baby!' Henry's eyes opened wide.

'Henry,' she looked into his eyes, 'do you not understand? Even if it is still inside me it will be dead.' She put her hand in the pot and moved it around in the liquid, drawing out a blob that fitted in the palm of her hand.

'Look Henry, that's our baby's sac.'

'What do you mean?'

'It's like a bag. The baby lived in it while it was inside me.'

'What? How do you know?'

'All animals do it. My Ma showed me when one of the sheep lost a lamb.'

'She poked around in what came out of a sheep and made you look at it! Ugh, that's horrible.'

'No, it's not. It's just nature. She was teaching me. My Ma can't read or write and they needed me to help on the farm so I couldn't go to school and didn't learn the things which you did. She taught me what she knew about the world around her. When she showed me the tiny lamb she told me then that I had lived in a bag like that inside her and that my children would live in the same way inside me.'

'S-so our baby is in there. Why has it not stayed inside you?'

'Ma said that sometimes something goes wrong and the birth happens before the baby is able to live.' She looked at him while he put the pot down. 'I'm sorry, perhaps I should not have shown you. I don't think my Ma ever told my Pa. Perhaps it is something that only women should hear.' Henry shook his head.

'I'm glad you've told me. I am amazed at the things you know.' He pulled her to him and wrapped his arms around her. 'It would have been another of our children and now it is a small blob in the piss pot.' He shook his head at the thought.

It was quiet for a few moments. Mary-Ann pulled herself away from him slightly.

'You say "it". We could look and see if it was a girl or a boy.' She spoke quietly and her eyes scanned his face. Henry's mouth opened and his eyes widened as she continued, 'Help me sit on the bed. Then I'll hold the sac while you take the piss pot down and empty it. Put some clean water in it and bring it back here. I'll open the sac in the water and try to find the baby. If it is alright I will show you if you want to see or I can just look and tell you what it is. My Ma told me that sometimes it is malformed and if it is don't look.' Henry studied his wife's face for a few moments. What she had just suggested ricocheted around his brain. Then he nodded slowly.

'Y-yes I think I would like to see.' He returned with the fresh water and sat next to her on the bed. He looked at what she was doing but couldn't see much because she had her hands under the surface of the water. Then she drew them out and he could see she had something in her hand. She lifted it near to her eyes.

'It was a boy,' she said. She turned her face to him and he nodded slowly. She brought her hand towards his face and he saw a small figure.

'If you look closely you can see his boy part.' Henry nodded, unable to speak for a few moments.

'He a baby but just very small,' he croaked, his voice thick with emotion, 'Beautiful.' He turned to her and there were tears in his eyes. 'Why did he die?'

'I can't tell you that. Ma used to tell the women in the village that God was saving their child from a tragedy. She said that she thought that God could see some terrible thing would happen if the child lived so he made the birth happen early so it would die.'

'You'd think that God could stop the terrible thing happening and let him live,' spluttered Henry. Mary-Ann put her hand on his arm and kissed his cheek.

'It has happened to this child but there will be others. When I stop bleeding...' She smiled at him and he smiled back.

'I'll bury him in the back yard,' he said, 'we can't...' They both shook their heads. When a child was stillborn it was normal to find someone who was having a funeral and ask if the body could be placed in the coffin but they knew that people would be horrified at what they had just done. 'It's strange. If you hadn't shown me I would happily have poured the contents of the piss pot into the privy but I can't now.' She handed the small body to him and he went. She cleaned herself and dressed, putting plenty of rags in her underwear to soak up the bleeding. She was just coming down the stairs with the children when she heard an agitated knocking on the front door. Tom, who had been in the living room eating his breakfast, reached the door first. He opened it.

'Where's Henry?' James looked grim.

'I'm here,' Henry replied from where he'd just entered from the back yard. He stopped when he saw James. 'It's Martha, isn't it? She's bad again. I'll come with...' James was shaking his head.

'I'm sorry. We thought she was sleeping late. Hannah went to try and wake her but she was already cold. It must have happened early in the night.' Henry slumped against the wall and Mary-Ann sat on the stairs. Louisa sat down next to her whilst the younger ones played on the floor, childishly noisy and unaware. Henry shook his head.

'Like she said that day when the doctor asked her – she tried her best not to die,' he said. He was shaking and Tom saw it.

'I think you need to sit down,' he said as he led Henry through to the living room. James followed them.

'I'm sure we can manage without you at the yard. Freddie and Jim can sort out Bessie. I'll tell Robert.' Henry nodded.

'I'll be there later.' James left with Tom. Mary-Ann put the children in the pen and turned to Henry.

'I think we could both do with some hot, sweet tea,' she said as she went through to the kitchen. When she'd moved the kettle to the fire she sat next to Henry on the bench and hugged him.

'So much has happened.'

'Martha – she hurt so much and was so brave. Only yesterday when I visited her on my way home I thought she was beginning to put weight back on and there was some colour in her cheeks. She was on the way to being well and then she just dies in her sleep. It doesn't seem fair.'

'But that's how it is. Perhaps it would have been kinder if the water had taken her although drowning must be dreadful – choking and not being able to breathe.'

'Another death because of that bridge. Another one of my father's children.'

'Now you cannot blame yourself for this.' Mary-Ann pulled him towards her and stroked his head.

'Perhaps if I'd warned them, called out after them as they followed that silly clown. I knew that bridge was unsafe.' Mary-Ann said nothing but just hugged him tighter. They stayed still and unspeaking for a few minutes until Louisa and Carrie started to squabble which made Harry cry.

'They are hungry,' said Mary-Ann. 'None of us has eaten yet this morning and that kettle's boiling.'

'After we have eaten I'll take myself to the yard. It's easier if I'm busy.'

Martha was buried next to Maria two days later. After the funeral Henry did not return home with his family. It was June and by the time the sun set Mary-Ann was worried. She was ready for bed when Robert and James helped him home. He was inebriated and slept downstairs in his chair.

11

'The Mayor has declared the town's official mourning for the bridge disaster to be over and has announced that the water frolic at Burgh will happen as usual,' said James one morning in the week after Martha's funeral. Robert, James and Henry were standing by the cottage door whilst the men stood around Bessie with their morning tea. Robert drew a deep breath.

'I suppose the town has had its fill of sadness. I propose that we all go together, as a family. What do you think, Henry?'

'It seems so soon after putting Martha into the ground – the earth will not even have settled around her yet,' he said, his head bowed, 'but if the rest of the town is ready to smile and if my Mary-Ann is happy with it, we will come. The children will enjoy it.' When he looked up he was smiling.

Saturday the twenty-sixth of July dawned fair and the Spandler family met at the yard at eight o'clock. The King's Arms was using the horse which they shared but they had their own cart. Upon it was a large crate in which had been put a layer of straw on top of which was a pan of mutton stew made by Mary, Robert's wife. Henry and Tom lifted their contribution into the crate: a large pan of potatoes and onions. The day before Mary-Ann had rendered bacon fat from the flitch which hung from a hook on the inside of the chimney and in this fried a large quantity of onions. That morning she'd boiled potatoes and added them, and some of their cooking liquid, to the fried onions. She stirred them together and left them on the edge of the fire to stay hot until they were ready to leave. As Henry and his family approached Mary crossed over Northgate with a large basket full of bread from Boulters. Shortly after James and Hannah arrived with a pan of turnips mixed with a few early carrots. This was placed in the crate before heavy lumps of wood were placed on top of the lids of each of the pans and more straw was packed round and on top of them. The lid of the crate was secured and covered with an old blanket. James and Hannah also brought a large earthenware pot and when the rest of the family caught sight of it they cheered, knowing that it would contain pickled radish, a favourite. This was placed alongside the crate.

They set off. At the front was the cart, around which the men were grouped, and Richard and George, the younger sons of Robert and James, pulled it across White Horse Plain. However, they were young and still at school so had not developed the strength that would come once they started at the yard. Therefore, as they turned down Fuller's Hill, others helped them to stop the weight of the cart pulling it out of their control. Half way down the hill they turned into George Street. This was a gentler slope down to the quay and they were allowed to guide the cart on their own. The family were making their way to a field near the old Roman fort of Burgh Castle which overlooked Breydon Water. During the next two hours most the men took turns in pulling, with the exception of Edmund who was perspiring heavily and red in the face.

They reached the drawbridge and crossed over to Southtown. Behind the men the children ran and played as they walked along, with the women behind them to make sure none were lost. As they crossed the bridge Mary-Ann noticed Mary, Robert's wife, glance at the water and close her eyes. She put a hand on her arm. Mary turned to her and at that moment, Harry, who was strapped to Mary-Ann's back now that he was bigger, looked at her from behind his mother's head and smiled, inducing Mary to smile in return.

'You and your Ma make me feel better,' she said to him. Harry jiggled up and down and banged his hands on Mary-Ann's back. Mary-Ann grinned and turned her head to see him.

'Yes, and wriggle like that much more and you will be down from there and walking on your own legs – although that will slow us down.'

'Carrie's managing to keep up with Louisa and Martha-Ann,' said Mary, nodding towards the girls.

'They're growing, your little ones,' said Hannah, James's wife. Mary and Rachel, Henry's sisters were walking with them. They looked at each other.

'We'll take a turn at carrying him if he becomes heavy for you,' said Rachel.

'That's kind of you,' said Mary-Ann. 'By the time we have the first rest I'll be more than happy for you to take him.' This was at a mill in Southtown which had a maintenance contract with the Spandlers. The family was well known to them. Adults sat upon walls, tree stumps and grassy banks whilst the children continued to run around for a few minutes until one by one they all flopped to the ground. They rested for about fifteen minutes before moving on again. The second stop was at Bradwell Farm where the farmer's wife filled a barrel with water for them. It was nearly noon by the time they arrived at the castle and found a place on the Burgh Flats at the foot of the hill upon which the ruins stood. There were already many people there. Robert and James found where the King's Arms had set up and bought two flagons of ale. Meanwhile Mary and Hannah found a lemonade seller who filled up the three large jugs they'd brought. The crate was opened and the pans of food were removed and set on the edge of the cart from where the families helped themselves. Rachel passed between them with the basket of bread so that everyone could take some. As they finished eating Robert raised his voice to get everyone's attention.

'Mary and I want to be back at South Quay in time for the rowing races because our Robert is taking part so I'd like us to leave as soon as the last race finishes here, before the presentations.' A hubbub followed until they noticed Robert and Mary talking together and it went quiet again.

'They're usually dull anyway,' Freddie called out.

'Yes, and it will be good to cheer on young Robert,' added Jim.

'Shush,' called several people as Robert looked round.

'Mary says I'm to tell you that she has made Nelson cake,' he announced. This was a fruit cake made from stale bread which had been soaked before mixing with butter, egg, dried fruit and spices and baking in the oven. Everyone cheered. 'She suggests we save it for later and eat it at the quayside.' People nodded their heads in agreement.

'I'm so full I would have to force it down,' called Tom. Everyone laughed: his appetite was known by all. Henry noticed Edmund heave himself to his feet and go and look in the pans, turning away with a shrug and a scowl, before walking over to Robert and Mary. Henry edged closer so that he could hear above the other voices.

'Ma, my friends are over there.' He pointed and Henry saw the group in the corner of the field where the King's Arms were selling ale. 'Can I take my piece of cake and go and join them?'

'Er…' Mary faltered as she looked at Robert.

'No-one else is having it now,' he pointed out. 'I think you can wait until we're by the quay like everyone else.'

'But I'm still hungry.' Robert caught Henry's eye and raised his eyes to the sky as Edmund continued, 'I don't want to watch the rowing races. I want to stay here.' Edmund folded his arms across his chest and pouted.

'That fine, I'm sure we'll find someone else to eat your share of the cake – although I seem to remember seeing you in the kitchen this morning whilst Ma was cutting it up and your mouth was rather full then. If you want cake this afternoon you will need to come with us.' Edmund snorted and walked away. Henry wondered what he would do.

'Look, there's the mayor in his boat,' shouted James, 'you can see the sun glinting on his chain.'

'Where?' called several people.

'There. His boat has just come out of the river.' He pointed towards Breydon Water where the rivers Bure and Yare met each other. 'It's the largest of the boats, the one decorated with all the flowers.'

'Look at all the little boats following it,' called someone else. When the official procession had passed by some of the other boats turned back.

'They're getting ready for the races,' called Freddie, 'I'm going to watch that small blue one.'

'And I'll watch the green one,' countered his brother, Jim, 'it's about the same size as yours. I bet mine will win!' During the races Burgh Flats was a scene of much merriment as the townsfolk of Yarmouth cheered and laughed.

'I can remember Maria talking about this in the middle of winter when we were cold. She told me how much fun it was and said how she liked the pretty boats,' said Mary-Ann to Henry.

'Yes, and Martha would have enjoyed today as well,' he replied, 'but look at Louisa and Carrie playing with Martha-Ann – it's good to see them well. I still feel really sad when I think about the bridge and all those people but I'm being happy today. It's the same with my Ma and Pa and all the deaths then – the past has happened and I can't change it now.' They heard the bang of a gun as another race started and everyone round them started shouting at the boats on the water. Mary-Ann and Henry looked at each other, laughed and joined in.

'We'll make quicker time going back if the children ride in the cart,' suggested Robert at the end of the last race. 'Take the straw out of the crate and cover it with the blanket then they can sit on that,' he said as the pans were replaced ready for the return journey.

'Louisa, Carrie, up you climb,' called Henry. He noticed Edmund standing further back talking to Mary.

'Hold onto him tightly,' Mary-Ann told Louisa as she put Harry on her lap, 'although I think he'll be asleep before we leave the field he's been running around so much.' Mary came and said something quietly in Robert's ear which Henry couldn't hear: however, when Robert glanced sharply at his son and shook his head Henry guessed what had been asked. Edmund saw Henry watching and scowled at him. As they made their way back to South Quay Henry walked with his younger brother, Tom, and Jim and Freddie, the sons of James.

'Ed's falling a long way behind,' noticed Freddie.

'Yes,' said Henry, 'I think he wanted to ride in the cart with the children but his father said no.'

'I should think not,' retorted Tom, 'he's older than any of us – well except you Henry.' He grinned at his brother.

'Mmm, I think he is really finding it difficult, not just being lazy,' Henry pointed out.

'Perhaps if he didn't eat so much. He's so fat it must be like carrying several iron bars all the time. I'm sure he's bigger than ever – his backside certainly wobbles more!'

'It must make it harder,' admitted Henry, 'but I remember when he was a young boy he was always out of breath and that was before he was fat.'

'Talking of Ed makes me gloomy,' said Jim, 'I try not to think about what it will be like when there is just us left, when our Pa and Uncle Robert are dead. I wish Pa was the elder then I would become the master-in-charge. You would be the best,' he turned to Henry who nodded and shrugged his shoulders, 'but I know I would be better than Ed.'

'Do you not think a day passes when I don't think of how it could have been?' asked Henry. His voice had an edge that severed the conversation.

At South Quay they found Hannah and Elizabeth, the sisters of Robert and James, who had elected not to walk to Burgh and were waiting by the quayside to see their nephew in his race. Mary opened a hamper and took out trays of cake which were handed around. Henry noticed that she kept looking in the direction from which they'd come. Eventually

Edmund caught up with them and Henry watched as she gave him two slices of cake which she had saved for him. Half an hour later and the first of the rowing races had just finished when Robert approached him.

'Have you seen Edmund? He seems to have disappeared.'

'I saw him arrive sometime after us,' Henry replied, 'but I've not noticed him since.'

'It's our Robert's race soon and Mary was wondering where he was. She thought he would want to be with us to watch his brother.' Henry looked at Robert with raised eyebrows but didn't comment. James approached.

'Apparently Jim and Freddie saw him heading off towards the Coalmeter's Tavern,' he said. Robert grimaced and went off to re-join Mary for the race.

'I don't think that pleased him,' commented Henry.

'No, nor Mary.' Henry glanced towards Robert and Mary. She was pointing towards the tavern but Robert was shaking his head.

'What do you think, James? You're Robert's brother – does he realise that Ed is never going to mature? That he'll never improve enough to be master-in-charge?'

'I think he still hopes. I know he's spent some evenings in the work room with him recently, although I'll be amazed if it makes much difference. I know I tried to help Ed learn but he seems to be incapable of it. What's worse is that, as the son of the master-in-charge, he seems to think it is unnecessary for him!'

At that point shouting erupted around them as Robert's race started and James and Henry joined in the cheering. Henry was fascinated to watch Robert rowing: his movements were fluid and co-ordinated in contrast to how Henry remembered him in the year he had spent as an apprentice in the yard.

'He's second!' James declared as the race finished. 'I think the winner was Steven, one of his shipmates. He introduced me at the cottage last night.'

'Robert must be pleased to see his eldest son succeed,' said Henry. James frowned but Henry shook his head. 'No, I don't mean coming second in the race – I mean his chosen craft. Do you know young Robert is now second mate on his ship? He could never have been a good millwright he was too clumsy but he's found something he can do and has left the yard behind. It's a pity that Ed can't find something at which he can excel.' It was James's turn to shake his head.

'Robert and I are not the same but most people can see that we're brothers. Young Robert and Edmund are quite different from each other. As Robert's eldest son Robert could have stayed at the yard and waited until he became master-in-charge, much as Ed is doing but he didn't.'

'Ed isn't spirited enough to do anything like Robert,' Henry replied, 'the others were talking about him as we walked from Burgh. Perhaps he can't because he doesn't breathe properly – it must make it hard – although it could be that he's just too lazy.' He shrugged. 'I don't know why he is like he is but I know that if he does not change it will be bad for the yard when you and uncle Robert have gone.' James looked sharply at him and the two men lapsed into silence.

'Who checked these?' asked Freddie a week later while they were unloading a new order of tree trunks from the cart.

'Well it certainly wasn't me,' Henry grimaced. 'Look at how mis-shapen that one is. We might make a few cogs from it but it'll mostly go to firewood!' Just then Robert came out of the cottage, strode past them and disappeared down the passage to the gate. He did not make eye contact with anyone and his face was grim.

'Looking at him I think I can guess,' said Tom.

'Yes, you're probably right,' replied Henry, 'but I'm puzzled. Not even Ed is stupid enough to accept these.' Freddie turned to go down the passage.

'Come on, there's still a few more to un...' Robert rounded the corner and nearly ran into him.

'Where is he?' His face was dark with rage as he looked from one to the other of them. 'Edmund – where is he?' His eyes roved around the yard.

'I saw him about ten minutes ago,' Freddie replied. 'He called me over from where I was working and said that the wood was outside. I followed him out and he went to start unhitching the horse so I came back in here to find help to unload. When we got outside he had gone.' Robert stormed off into the cottage. A few moments later, as the last of the wood was carried into the yard, James appeared from the cottage. Henry looked at him and raised his eyebrows.

'Ed accepted these trunks? I didn't think even he would have done that.'

'It seems so. I've told Robert that we need to meet together and discuss the future of the yard. After we close in the King's Arms?'

'I could come but surely it's not for me to discuss?'

'Henry, in spite of your position – or perhaps even because of it – you need to be there. In the future you will not inherit but the yard is important to you. Besides which I want your opinion at the discussion. It will be hard. I've told Robert I'm asking you but he said that none of the others were to come.'

Henry stared into his tankard of ale as he waited for his uncles to arrive. He couldn't stop himself musing on how things could have been so different if his father had not been so foolish. Edmund would then have just been an irritation, a nuisance that he would have to deal when he became master-in-charge. That is what he would have been, in the end, if his father had not sold his share and lost his inheritance. He gripped his tankard tightly as he thought of his father. Damn him, did he care so little about the yard that he was prepared to lose it for the possibility of becoming a rich man? He'd known that he was about to become master-in-charge. Why was that not enough for him? Henry wondered what his father would have been like as he became older and how it would have been. He had memories of the early years of his apprenticeship when he and his father had worked alongside each other and a smile stole onto his face.

'What are you amusing yourself with?' asked James. Henry jumped at his uncles as they sat down.

'I was just visualising what it would be like working with my father if he were still alive.'

'Would that he was,' said Robert. 'My Edmund may have turned out differently if he had. His Ma pictures her son as the master-in-charge in years to come and often tells him how wonderful that will be. I tell her when things go wrong, like this morning...'

'What happened?' Henry asked, 'I am surprised Ed accepted that wood – he knows better than that.'

'And he probably would not have done had he been there when it was unloaded.'

'But he was out of the yard all morning?'

'He says he grew tired waiting by the quay for the ship to arrive. Then he saw one of his friends who suggested they went for a tankard. Then he says he forgot...'

'Forgot?' demanded James, raising his voice. 'He forgot?' Others in the tavern turned to look at James. Henry shook his head: James was mild-mannered and he'd rarely heard him raise his voice. Robert nodded.

'When he remembered and arrived at the quay he found the ship and the merchant gone and a young lad watching the wood. Fortunately for him his friend helped him load it onto the cart.'

'Robert,' said James, quietly now, 'I don't think that there will be a yard after Ed takes over.'

'I know – and I'm worried.' Robert looked at his ale and no-one spoke for a few moments

'We were talking about Ed on the way back from Burgh,' said Henry, 'and I have thought of a way which would stop Ed being master-in-charge.' The two older men stared at Henry as he continued, 'and I feel I can suggest this because I will not gain from it myself.' He drew a deep breath. 'If you were to sell your share so that James became master-in-charge then Jim would inherit the position. Ed would inherit your money but not the yard.' Robert shook his head.

'I can't do that because we would then have to leave the cottage and my Mary would be upset – and she thinks I'm unfair to Edmund now. She would have apoplexy if I tried to sell.'

'But what of the yard?' Henry insisted.

'Edmund is young yet,' Robert reasoned. Henry looked at James but his face remained impassive. He turned back to Robert.

'Do you think he can improve? He doesn't have the ability to be a millwright and he thinks the work is unimportant, not worthy of his full atten…' Henry stopped as Robert's shoulders slumped and he put his head in his hands. James put an arm on his shoulder.

'I don't want the position for myself, or even for my boys,' James said quietly, 'and I certainly don't want to evict you from the cottage.' No-one spoke. Then Robert sat up and looked straight ahead, his lips thin and pressed together.

'Ten years. I'm only fifty-five. I'll give him ten years. If he has not changed, I will do as you suggest.'

'What of young Richard?' suggested James, 'he seems a lively lad.' Robert nodded.

'Only nine now but in ten years he will be nineteen and if needs be I will put it in my will that he is to be the next master-in-charge. I still hope Edmund will prove himself by then.' Seeing Robert's distress Henry also put an arm on his shoulder.

'We hope so as well.'

'I think that you need to talk to Mary,' said James, his voice soft and measured, 'because she needs to see him as he is.'

'And to treat him differently,' added Henry. 'Do you know that she'd saved him two pieces of the Nelson cake when he arrived at the quay on the day of the frolic? It would help him if he didn't eat so much. I'm sure I would be breathless if I was that large.' Robert nodded.

'Only last week Mary was complaining I never gave him important jobs to do.'

'Perhaps after today's debacle she will see why.' suggested James.

'She insists he's ill. I called the doctor last week and was hoping he would agree with me but after he sounded his heart he said that there was something wrong with it. Now she's overcome with motherly feelings towards him and won't let him lift a finger indoors. She thinks I ought to put him in charge of the office.' James looked horrified.

'But his hand is so poor it's hard to read what he writes – and he cannot reckon.' Robert snorted.

'Yes, I know that.'

'Did the doctor say anything about his diet?'

'Yes, he did tell Mary not to feed him so much but I haven't noticed his plate being any less full since.' James looked closely at his brother.

'Robert, if you want Edmund to be your successor you must sit down with both of them and tell them how things must change – not discuss it but tell them. Insist. And at the yard he must go back to the work room until he learns to understand the craft. Even if he is not going to be able to physically do the work he has to understand the principles behind it and you must be the teacher. I tried, I tried very hard with him when he was my apprentice.'

'I regret now saying he had finished his apprenticeship and declaring him to be a millwright,' said Robert. He did not look at either of the other men but instead studied his hands. 'He complained that he was older than you'd been when you finished.'

'That was completely different, Henry was ready,' declared James.

'Yes, but his Ma said I was being unfair.' James turned so that he could look directly into Robert's eyes.

'Robert, his Ma is not the master-in-charge, you are. I remember telling you I was not happy with Edmund finishing his apprenticeship but you insisted. You need to insist more in your home. I would advise you to tell him that he is no longer a millwright until he has proved himself. Make him learn or face the fact that he cannot be master-in-charge.'

Henry looked from one to the other of his uncles. He had made his suggestion but now said nothing. His mind was whirling.

12

It was the end of August. Mary-Ann had been to the market and when she returned she prepared something for Carrie and Harry to eat. Eventually she made herself something but by then she felt queasy. She spent the afternoon putting new cuffs on one of Henry's old shirts. When she stopped to make herself some tea she stared unseeing while the kettle boiled remembering that it was Friday, the day Maria used to come and visit. She was drinking her tea when six-year-old Louisa, her cheeks red from running, came in from school. It occurred to her that her tea tasted odd.

'Have you been running with the boys again? You know what your Pa said. You're a girl and he wants you to grow up a young lady.' Louisa shrugged and pulled a face. 'Go and take your school clothes off. Hang them up so that they don't become creased – you don't want to be spoken to at school tomorrow. Your house clothes are on your bed.' Louisa skipped off up the stairs and Mary-Ann returned to her sewing. She tried her tea again and decided that she didn't like it. Louisa came downstairs with one of her school books, sat up at the table and started to read.

'Keep an eye on Carrie and Harry while I go and start the dinner.' Louisa looked up and nodded before returning to her book. Mary-Ann went into the small kitchen and poured some water into a bowl from a jug under the sink. She reached into a basket and drew out a bundle which she unwrapped: it contained fish heads and other scraps which she'd bought on the market that morning. Although they were fresh, as she dropped them into the water the smell made her retch. She stood still and, in a moment, realised that she had not bled since the miscarriage. She felt her breasts and they were slightly tender. She smiled but decided that she would not tell Henry yet.

'Well the vicar seemed pleased at the town's offerings this morning,' commented Henry as they were walking back from Sunday service at St Nicholas's.

'Yes, he said that God's wrath would be turned away because the poor will learn at school that they need to come and worship. As if the disaster was the fault of the poor!' Mary-Ann's voice was raised in indignation.

'It's an amazing amount of money that's been raised,' stated Tom, 'and in such a short time as well.'

'I would think much of it came from the wealthy of Yarmouth,' suggested Henry.

'And so it should,' retorted Mary-Ann. 'The poor haven't money to spare for building schools and churches. Perhaps if the rich had given before, then God would not have been angry.'

'It will be good for the poor when the school is built though,' suggested Tom.

'Maybe but it depends whether they have to pay for it. Even if they only expect the children to bring a penny it will be too much for some families – why, if they have six children it would be a tanner a week,' Mary-Ann glanced at Tom and Henry, 'and those children would have to stop working so they wouldn't earn anything. The family would have to choose between school or food.'

'Apparently some of the money is to be used to open up the church again so they're going to take down those walls that you think are so odd Mary-Ann,' said Henry.

'I look forward to seeing that,' said Mary-Ann, 'it will wonderful. A huge space like that will fill a person with awe. It will be a good place to worship God in.'

At the beginning of October Mary-Ann was still being sick and, on some mornings, had to dash out to the privy as soon as she came downstairs. She was amazed that Henry had not noticed. Although she disliked the discomfort she was reassured by it: she'd realised, after she'd miscarried, that she'd stopped feeling sick in the week after the bridge disaster. As this baby was still making her sick, she felt everything was well. That night in bed she wriggled close to Henry so that he put his arm around her and began tracing his finger down her face.

'You're smiling,' he said as he reached her lips. He leant towards her and kissed her gently.

'That's because I'm happy,' she replied as he moved his finger down to her nightdress and started to undo the buttons. 'You know sometimes I wonder why I bother to do those up.' Henry chuckled.

'It's because you want to make me work for my pleasures,' he said as he slipped beneath the fabric and cupped her breasts, 'but it's certainly worth the effort. I like to feel the weight of them in my hands.'

'And are they heavier than usual?' Henry stopped fondling.

'Why?'

'Because they are preparing to make milk for your next child,' she said, her voice singing with pleasure. Henry lay still and quiet.

'I hope it will be alright,' he whispered.

'It's still making me feel sick so I'm sure it's fine. It should be born around Easter.' Henry hugged her closely.

'I was going to come into you but I don't think I want to anymore.'

'I'd like you to. You will not disturb the babe.'

'Perhaps I did, last time.'

'No. If anything it may have been the shock of Maria's death. I do miss her.' Henry tightened his hold on her. 'I still want you to love me though. I don't want to miss that as well.'

'I'll be gentle.'

'Like you used to when we were first together? Do you remember I told you that my Ma sat on me and bounced up and down to try and dislodge Louisa? She made me cry but it didn't hurt the baby.'

The men were standing around Bessie with their tea as they'd done every morning since Robert had been master-in-charge.

'It's stormy out there. Blowing a gale,' said Tom as he and Henry came out of the passage which led from the yard door.

'It's a high tide as well,' said Mr Gough, 'and the Bure has burst its banks. It's lapping up the bottom of our Row. I'm told that at t'Trinity Arms down Southgate customers have taken to boats and have moored outside. They're served through t'window!'

'Well they'll continue to trade if they can,' said Tom, 'it's quiet in here though.'

'It may not stay that way. If there's any so foolish as to work their mill we'll have plenty to keep us busy before Christmas,' cautioned Henry.

'But we've to prepare the yard for the Christmas feast,' objected Edmund.

'Well you'd best be doing it now,' said James, 'because Henry's right. We may have no time for making the yard look festive if they've tried to carry on milling.' Edmund scowled and heaved himself to his feet from the bench where he'd been sitting. Around him were some of the younger apprentices who looked at each other as Edmund wobbled before them. Henry noticed some of them smirking.

'Pa has tasked me with finding greenery,' he said, looking around. No-one met his eyes. 'I'm off to the lanes to see what's growing in the ditches.' One of the younger lads stood.

'I'll come with you,' he said. Tom looked at them before he too stood up.

'If there are no tasks for me here,' he said, looking at James who shook his head, 'I'll come and help you. I like the yard to look green at Christmas as much as anyone.' Edmund looked surprised. 'Let's look in at the store and see if there are any sacks we can use to bring it back,' Tom continued.

'That's a good idea, Tom,' Edmund beamed at him, 'thank-you.' As they left James turned to Henry.

'I see young Tom is as caring as his elder brother,' he said. Henry blushed. Robert came out of the cottage towards him.

'Henry,' he said, 'I've had a letter from a Mr Corp. Apparently he knows Mr Turner.' Henry frowned. 'Don't you remember – William, the tailor?'

'Eliza!' exclaimed Henry. 'She left so long ago and so much has happened that I'd almost stopped thinking about her. You've had a letter from someone that knows him? Did he mention Eliza? Is she alright?'

'He says she's in good health. He writes about Mary.'

'Mary? Our Mary, my sister?' Robert nodded.

'Yes, he knows Eliza and would like to meet her sister. He is quite clear in his intentions. If she is as pleasant as he finds Eliza to be he will propose marriage.'

'And what is his position?'

'Much the same as your own. He is a millwright employed at a yard in Yorkshire. His master-in-charge is a friend of Mr Turner.' Henry nodded.

'It sounds like he will be able to provide for my sister, at least as well as I provide for Mary-Ann. So, when is he coming – and does Mary know?'

'Not yet. I wondered if you'd like to be the one who tells her?'

'Yes, that would be good. I will miss her when she goes.'

'Nothing definitely decided. He may meet her and change his mind,' Robert paused and chuckled, 'although I cannot see how anyone could find anything to object about. She is a lovely young woman and your Pa and Ma would have been proud of her.' Mary was happy when Henry told her and, although she was sad at the thought of leaving the family in

Yarmouth, she looked forward to seeing Eliza again. The two girls had become close, working together in the dark years after their father went to London and returned a broken man.

It was December. Robert stepped up onto one of the benches at the yard and the family, who had gathered for the Christmas eve celebration, fell silent. He smiled.

'When my father bought this yard and I and my brothers and sisters were young I can remember playing here.' His hand traced an arc as he indicated the space in which they stood. 'There was one bench then and an open fire which we were warned to stay away from.' He looked at his brother James and glanced at his sisters. 'He would have been proud to see you all today.' At that moment Harry saw Martha-Ann, giggled, and ran across the yard to her. Robert laughed. 'And to hear the next generation of Spandlers making themselves noticed.' He stopped for a moment and drew a deep breath. 'It is sad that two of the younger ones have gone on to meet him before their time.' His voice cracked and he looked at Henry. Edmund, who had been watching his father until that moment, looked away. No-one spoke as Robert stepped down from the bench. Conversations were starting up again when someone was heard to be knocking at the door of the yard. Robert indicated to Edmund to see to them and everyone was quiet again as he went. When he returned down the passage from the gate, followed by Ned who carried his fiddle, everyone cheered.

Henry picked up a plate of food and went and stood with Mary, Tom and Rachel.

'These pies are good,' he said. Rachel beamed.

'Old Aunt Elizabeth told me that I should have made one large rectangular one because she said that was the tradition.'

'I remember the old way,' replied Henry. 'It was always big and had to be cut up so everyone could have some. Then the mincemeat filling would fall out of the side when you picked up a piece.' They all laughed. The fiddler started to play and they looked in his direction as Louisa and Carrie ventured near him to watch. When he saw his young audience he took a small bow and started to jig. The two girls giggled and copied him. Henry caught Mary-Ann's eye and they both smiled at each other.

'My intended is coming after Christmas,' said Mary and Henry pulled his eyes from Mary-Ann to look at her. Then she chuckled. 'Apparently his name is Christmas. Christmas Corp!'

'There are some in the town whose surname is Christmas,' said Rachel, 'but I've never heard it as a given name.'

'Perhaps his family came from here,' suggested Tom.

'Or they could have left behind some good friends whose surname was Christmas, so they decided to give it to their son,' added Rachel. 'We'll miss you but I'm sure Eliza will be happy that you're coming.'

'I think Eliza is prettier than I am, so he may be disappointed and decide he doesn't want me. Then you won't need to miss me!' Mary laughed.

'It'll be exciting for you – new people to meet and a new town to find your way around,' said Tom.

'I'm not sure about that,' retorted Mary.

'At least Eliza will be there, so you will know somebody,' said Henry. Mary nodded but she knew, as they all did, that it would depend on how near they were and whether the families met together: Eliza was married to a master tailor and Christmas was simply an employee at a millwrights' yard. Rachel, seeing the apprehension in Mary's eyes, gave her a hug. When their parents died the two sisters had been sent to live with their aunt, Hannah, who was the sister of Robert and James, and over the past eight years had become very close.

At five foot seven Mary was exceptionally tall for a woman at that time: she was almost as tall as her brother

Henry. Christmas finally arrived at the end of January, his visit being delayed by heavy snow. His appearance caused consternation in the Spandler family: he was a small man and only came up to Mary's shoulder so that it looked peculiar when they stood together. He stayed for a few days which he spent at the yard looking at the work being done and sharing techniques from his yard in Yorkshire. In the evenings he went to the home where Mary and Rachel lived with Hannah. On the last evening he formally proposed to her but told her that he didn't expect her to give him an answer until after he had left and she had spoken with her brother and uncles.

The day after he left Henry met with Robert and James.

'My Mary says that she should not go,' said Robert, 'that people will laugh when they see them together. It's making the family an object of mirth.'

'But he is well able to provide for her,' pointed out James. 'What does Mary think?'

'She says he seems to be kind and he's good company,' replied Henry. 'He makes her laugh and she thinks she could become fond of him.'

'What of his appearance?'

'She says it felt awkward at first, being taller than him, but that she hardly noticed by the time he left.'

'I have to say that his height was quite a shock when I first saw him,' stated Robert, 'but he certainly knew about the craft and his master's yard seems large and has plenty of work. She'll not be destitute. I say she should go.'

'I'm fairly sure Mary will be quite happy about that,' said Henry.

'And what of you? Are you happy? James asked him.

'Yes, it's not as good a position as she would have had if Pa had not gone and she had been the daughter of the master-in-charge, but I think she will be happy. I will miss her though and I think Rachel will be sad. She will be on her own with your sister Hannah when she's gone.'

'Yes, but unless she is very unfortunate she will not be there forever,' suggested Robert. 'She has turned into a lovely young woman and I'm sure it will not be long before she goes to make her own life as well.' He looked at Henry who was looking at the floor. James put a hand on his shoulder.

'Be of good cheer. Your sisters have lived to grow up and as women are going to live out their lives. You have to say farewell but be proud of who they are because it is your doing, because you were so strong when your father left.'

'She was strong as well. Without her and Eliza I couldn't have continued. But I am happy that she has found someone who will care for her and I hope Rachel is as fortunate.' He stopped and chuckled. 'Tom is still here – at least I have one brother who'll stay in Yarmouth with me.'

13

It was towards the end of March when Henry realised that all was not well. One evening he and Tom had come in from the day's work at the yard and were sitting with their tea while Mary-Ann finished cooking their food. As they talked her kept noticing her: once she grimaced as she stood up from her cooking pot and another time she put her hand into the small of her back and sighed.

'Are you alright?' She shook her head.

'It's this babe. I've never been this tired before and my back hurts. I shall be pleased when my time comes. It'll be easier then even if I do have another little one to look after.'

'I think I will go and see if your Ma can come.'

'No, not yet. I don't think this babe will come for a few weeks.'

'At the end of next week then. It can't be too busy at this time of year on the farm.'

'No – just the ploughing and the planting,' laughed Mary-Ann.

'I thought it was only during the harvest that it was busy.' Henry shrugged. 'I shall still go and see if she can come.' Mary-Ann nodded.

'It would be good to have her here. If you tell her how I've been she might bring something with her to help.'

Henry went for Abigail the following week. When she arrived she went straight up to the bedroom with Mary-Ann. When they came back downstairs Henry was not reassured by their faces.

'The babe is lying the wrong way inside me, Henry,' explained Mary-Ann.

'Tried t'turn it but wouldn't. I've seen them breech before and sometimes it's fine but then...' Abigail paused, 'but at least it's not sideways – that'd be really bad. Think I could feel a foot up by its head and if it stays like that it should slip out no trouble being as you already had several.'

It was the week after Easter. Henry and Tom were home from work and the children were in bed. Mary-Ann had paused several times while she and Abigail were clearing up after the evening meal. She went out to use the privy and leant on the door as she returned. She looked at her mother and nodded. Henry noticed.

'Have the pains started?' he asked his voice pitched higher than usual. Abigail nodded.

'Go upstairs, both of you,' she said. 'Mary-Ann, settle yourself in t'bed.'

'But Ma do you not need to put the soil sheet and the straw in to protect our mattress?'

'I've been watchin' you all day,' her mother replied. 'I knew you were startin' so I've already done it. Go and spend some time together now, while you can.' Henry's eyes widened but he did not comment as they went upstairs. As he had done during previous confinements, Tom left to sleep in the office at the yard. That night Henry dozed in one of the chairs.

'It's taking a long time but she's not too bad,' Abigail told him when she came downstairs the following morning, 'you could go up and see her afore you go out.' Henry was shocked to see how tired Mary-Ann looked. He kissed her before he left. Abigail insisted he went and he was happy to do so: he could not help and if he was busy at the yard he would not think about it too much and then perhaps it would all be alright. He left Louisa at school and took Carrie and Harry to the yard with him, leaving them at the cottage where it had been arranged for Mary, Robert's wife, to look after them. Tom had told them what was happening when he'd arrived at the cottage the previous evening.

'She started then?' Mary asked. Henry nodded, his face grim. 'The baby…?'

'No, it hasn't turned,' Henry informed her. 'I can tell that Abigail is worried although she keeps telling me all the reasons why Mary-Ann should be alright. But she is worried and hence so am I.'

'If when you go home tonight Abigail thinks she needs the doctor, then send for him,' ordered Robert. 'Do not worry about the fees because I will see to them.'

'Thank-you uncle,' said Henry. When the yard stopped for bread at midday, Henry went home. He opened the front door and heard Mary-Ann shouting out. He heard the pain in her voice and quickly retreated to the yard.

The time came to finish work for the day. Henry wanted to run home but at the same time he found many small tasks that needed doing. Tom found him.

'Come on, Henry, you must go back. I'll walk with you.'

'What if it's bad? What if it still isn't finished?'

'Then we will have to stay and listen or find somewhere else to go. I think if it had been really bad Abigail would have found someone walking past the house and asked them to call in here with a message.' Henry nodded.

They crept quietly into the house. Abigail was in the small kitchen. She smiled at them but they could see her fear in her eyes.

'They're both alive. You have a new son,' she said, nodding in the direction of the cradle near the fire, 'but both Mary-Ann and him are poorly. It took so long she hadn't much strength at the end. Thought he were dead at first so I put him t'one side because I didn't want to lose her as well but then I heard his little cry. He surprised me – he must've been determined t'live. She has lost a lot of blood...' Abigail faltered. Henry moved nearer to the cradle and looked at the sleeping baby. Abigail continued, 'he had a shaky start but he'll be okay. It's her I'm worried about. Go up to her, Henry, but don't wake her if she sleeps. She'll need all the rest she can get.'

A few moments later Henry reappeared.

'She's asleep. She looks so pale.' Abigail nodded.

'She's strong though. She's had food and shelter – not like the casuals on t'farm who move from place t'place, sleepin' in ditches and eatin' what they can catch or pick from the hedges. Some can't keep going like she's done today. She bled a lot but it was more like it should be the last time I looked. I have a special tea which helps and she can have it when this new boy of yours wakes t'feed.' Henry smiled and Abigail continued. 'It's good t'see you smile. You must, when she's awake. Talk to her about your new son. She must not see that we are worried.' Henry frowned. 'And, yes, I am. If she doesn't have another big bleed or come out in a fever in the next few days then she will live. But I warn you she will be weak for many weeks. I will need t'go back to the farm soon so you need t'find someone who can help her.' Henry nodded and went to the cradle. He picked up the baby.

'Your new grandson will be called William. Mary-Ann and I talked about it a few nights ago. He was my brother and died just before I met Mary-Ann.' Henry stopped stroked the baby's face and kissed his forehead. 'I hope your Ma's going to recover,' he whispered.

That night Henry stayed in the armchair again whilst his wife paused on the edge of death. A few times Abigail came downstairs. He looked at her but she only shook her head. Just before dawn he fell asleep but it was not a calm sleep. He dreamed: Mary-Ann was standing next to a coffin with her foot raised as if she was about to climb in. She smiled at him. He tried to shout, to run to her, but he could not utter a sound or move in any way. Someone pushed him, and he woke.

'She lives.' The statement was devoid of emotion. He stared at Abigail in confusion. 'She lives,' she repeated, 'go up and see her. She was awake as I left her.' Henry stood and shook away the night. Upstairs, Mary-Ann was pale and her eyes were closed. He thought she might have fallen asleep again so he sat next to her. The chair creaked and she opened her eyes. He stroked the hair from her forehead and was rewarded with the smallest of smiles.

'It was bad. I know,' he said softly, 'your Ma has told me. I have held William. Thank-you for giving me another son. I love you so much.'

'I love you,' she replied although her voice was so hoarse he could scarcely hear her. They sat in silence for several minutes until they heard the sound of footsteps on the stairs and a baby crying.

'His cry is weak,' said Abigail as she entered, 'but he is looking for food, which is good.' Henry took his new son from Abigail. The buttons to Mary-Ann's nightdress were already undone. He pulled the fabric down and stroked the baby's cheek with Mary-Ann's nipple. The baby turned and, finding what he was looking for, began to suck.

'You've done that before!' The tone in Abigail's voice expressed her surprise.

'Mary-Ann showed me with Carrie and I did it for Harry as well.' They both looked at Mary-Ann as she whimpered. Pain creased her face but Abigail smiled.

'Your womb is squeezing itself shut,' she said and, turning to Henry added, 'That's why it's hurting her so much.'

'B-But...' stuttered Henry.

'It's good. It happens when the baby feeds – helps to stop the bleeding.' Henry nodded uncertainly. This world of women perplexed him.

Tom returned a week later and by then Mary-Ann had recovered sufficiently to sit downstairs. Abigail declared that it was time for her to go back to the farm. After their shift at the silk factory on St Nicholas Road, Mary and Rachel came to visit.

'He's a lovely baby,' declared Rachel, who was holding him. Tom peeked over her shoulder.

'He's a baby, they're all the same.' The women all laughed while Tom shrugged.

'You'll say differently when it's your own child,' said Henry. He turned to his sisters. 'Did you know I'm taking Abigail back on Saturday?'

'We didn't but we'll ask at the factory and see if we can work our hours so that most of the time there is someone here to help you,' suggested Mary.

'Thank-you,' said Mary-Ann. She was still very pale. 'I'm enjoying having you all here. I was tired before you arrived.'

'Yes, your eyes kept closing and I think you slept for a while,' said Abigail.

'Well, we'll both enjoy coming and spending time with you,' said Mary. The girls looked at each other and nodded. She turned to Abigail, 'is there anything we need to know about Mary's care?'

'No,' said Abigail, 'now she just needs to eat well, rest and time will heal her. You will need to take over the care of the family though?' The question in Abigail's voice indicated her uncertainty.

'I can do that,' Mary assured her, 'and Rachel will help me. She looked after Tom when he was small.' She glanced at Henry and a cloud passed between them: they had done it before. 'We'll enjoy looking after your family, Henry.' She laughed and, as Henry's eyes flicked over his children and rested on his wife, the cloud dispersed.

In the week after Henry had taken Abigail back Robert made an announcement at the yard.

'I have decided that we'll have a small celebration at the end of the day today. I have asked the King's Arms to send some ale.'

'What are we celebrating, Pa?' Edmund asked. He had been in the workroom almost every evening since his father had spoken with him about his suitability as master-in-charge and told him that Richard might be appointed in his place; just yesterday had said he was pleased at how hard he was working. Edmund beamed. He was going to get his reward!

'Henry has a new son.' Everyone, except Edmund, cheered. 'We have disregarded it until now because it afflicted Mary-Ann almost to the grave.' The yard was unnaturally silent. 'However, this week she has revived.' There was a sigh as everyone let out a breath. Henry grinned. 'That, in view of the tragedy this family has borne this last twelve months, is worth rejoicing over.' Edmund reddened and sweat poured off him but no-one noticed. Robert went back into the cottage. Henry, Tom, Freddie and Jim were standing in a group and there was talk and laughter. Jim turned to one side just as Edmund approached.

'What's up Ed? You look agitated! Come and join us,' he said, smiling and indicating the group with his arm before he turned back to the conversation.' Edmund panted for a few moments.

'Congratulating the new father then are you?' he sneered. The conversation stopped as the other four glanced at each other before turning to stare at their cousin. 'I really don't know why you bother Henry – your children won't inherit the yard just like you won't.' As one the others turned back to each another and resumed their conversation. Jim turned his shoulder away from Edmund, excluding him from the group. Edmund pushed him.

'Listen to me,' he whined. With a nod of his head Henry indicated the far corner of the yard and they briskly walked over there, leaving Edmund staring after them. As they walked Henry noticed Robert and Mary standing in the door of the cottage. Mary was talking and pointing. Robert walked over to them.

'Mary has just watched Ed try and join your group but apparently after only a few words you've walked off and left him. She says that's what the problem is – you don't include him. She says he's very unhappy and that's why he eats so much.'

'So it's our fault that Ed is fat!' exclaimed Freddie.

'Uncle,' said Jim quietly, 'as Aunt Mary was watching she would have seen me smile at him and invite him to join us.' He indicated with his arm to Robert in the same way as he had with Edmund. 'He was angry before he joined us. He was frowning and his face was red. From where Mary was standing she could not hear what he said.'

'She told me that he had probably gone to congratulate you.' The whole group snorted.

'Robert, if she could have heard him she would have understood what actually happened,' said Henry. 'Far from congratulating me he told me I was wasting my time having children because they would have no inheritance.'

'We ignored him and it was then that he pushed Jim. We thought it was best to walk away from him.'

'I see,' said Robert, 'unfortunately he's probably already gone to his Ma with his own story. I wonder why he was already cross? I had just announced the celebration but I can't understand why it would be that.'

'Who knows,' said Freddie as Robert walked back to the cottage.

'Ed really does not like you,' stated Tom as he and Henry walked back to Francis Buildings after the celebration. 'Did you see the stare he gave you as Robert ushered him across the yard?' Henry nodded. Robert had decided that while Edmund did not wish to congratulate Henry he could spend the time doing extra theory in the workroom.

'Robert looked somewhat grim. I think there's been some hard words in that cottage.'

'It amused the younger apprentices,' said Tom with a chuckle, 'but then he does lord it over them.' Henry was silent for a few moments.

'It would have been hard enough, Pa having sold our share, to know that I was never going to hold the position I looked forward to holding as I grew up – but knowing it will go to Ed who will ruin the yard is dreadful.'

'Don't despair. The yard is all he has.'

'All?' Henry's eyebrows hid themselves in his hair which had fallen down over his forehead.

'Yes, all. He does not have a wife, especially one as comely as your Mary-Ann, and neither does he have children. I wonder whether that was why he was so vitriolic earlier. He may have the yard, but he knows he has no-one to inherit it from him.'

'But he's young yet,' shrugged Henry.

'Yes, and I'm sure he also knows that he will be completely unattractive to any daughter of all but the most desperate father,' counselled Tom. Henry chuckled, remembering the miller's daughter.'

'He will not like that!'

As they entered the house Rachel was lifting plates down from the rack and passing them to Louisa who was putting them on the table.

'The runner you sent told me you would be late,' she said over her shoulder, 'Aunt Hannah is going to have her meal with Uncle James tonight so I sent the runner on to the factory with a message for Mary to come and eat here. I've made a mutton stew for us all.' Henry rubbed his hands together in glee. Tom took the water bucket down to the well so he and Henry could wash away the day's grime and when they re-entered the house they found Mary had arrived and was helping Rachel put food on the plates.

'It's as well Uncle James made this table good and long when he gave it to us,' declared Henry as they all sat down. As he looked around the table he could not stop his face from smiling: Tom and his sisters with Mary-Ann and his children made it an animated mealtime. The children became very excited and were chattering so he quietened them all so they could eat. After the meal Mary sat at the table reading with Louisa whilst Tom and Rachel were on the floor with

Carrie and Harry playing with the wooden blocks which Tom had made from offcuts at the yard. Mary-Ann, in his mother's old chair, gently rocked herself whilst she darned some socks. She looked at Henry and they both smiled.

Mary-Ann was already in bed that night when William woke. Henry reached into the cradle and lifted him out. It always amazed him how strong, yet how fragile, a young baby was. William cried and wriggled in his hands. Henry leant over Mary-Ann and let him attach to a nipple before releasing him into Mary-Ann's arms. He climbed into bed and reached round her, supporting her with his arm while William suckled.

'Your Ma said he had a shaky start but he's certainly strong enough now,' he said as he watched his son.

'Our children are doing well,' she said, 'because you provide for us.

'And you have skills here in their home that keep them well. Look at how they enjoy their food.'

'Well it was your sister's cooking tonight! They're all growing. I know because I'm always needing to alter their clothes. I had to take the hem down on Louisa's dress again last week.'

'I hope she doesn't grow too tall. It will be good if the girls become women who are good company and pleasant to look upon.' He went quiet but then continued, 'what do you think our children will achieve in their lives? What sort of men will the girls marry and will the boys be good at the craft?' Mary-Ann chuckled.

'You're a wonder sometimes, Henry. There are many years to go before we need to think on such things.' She yawned. Henry stroked her hair.

'You've had a busy day.'

'I've done nothing,' she retorted. 'Your sister wouldn't let me. But yes, I'm tired.' He ran his finger down her nose.

'Has he finished?'

'Mmm.' Henry took his son from her and put him in his cradle.

'Sleep well. You're so precious to me.' He kissed her gently but she was already asleep. He lay staring into the darkness as his life ran through his mind: the happiness of his childhood; the excitement of growing up and the anguish of his early adult years all seemed so far away. He thought of the time after his parents died and he was on his own and knew that he could never have conceived of the level of happiness which he enjoyed now. For a moment he considered how good it would be to have the yard as well as his family until he realised that, had he been the son of the master-in-charge, he would not have considered Mary-Ann. The thought of not having her almost made his heart stop. Thoughts of the yard made him sad because he knew that, when Edmund became the master-in-charge, it would fail. He could still hear the pride in the voice of his grandfather when he was four and he'd lifted him up to the window in the office. They'd looked out at the yard where the men were all busy and he'd told him that, one day, he would be in charge but then it never happened because his father sold his share. His grandfather would be disappointed. Henry's fists tightened in frustration because he knew that he had all the abilities necessary to make the yard a success. But then Tom was right. He smiled as he thought of his wife and children and his fists uncurled. His breathing slowed. The yard would be his place of work and he would always enjoy the craft but he would live to see the achievements of his children. As he drifted off to sleep he thought of them.

As he slept he dreamed again but this time it was not of coffins. He was at a wedding and, in his dream, he couldn't work out why he was there because it was clearly a society wedding: there were too many people, the ladies wore plenty of jewellery and the clothes that were worn were fine and well-made. Then he realised he was coming down the aisle with a young woman on his arm. He turned to see which one of his daughters it was and at that point he woke up. It was his future: he would see his children advance in the world, he was sure of that. He snuggled closer to Mary-Ann and was still smiling when sleep reclaimed him.

38842880R00094

Printed in Poland
by Amazon Fulfillment
Poland Sp. z o.o., Wrocław